# Rosa of the Wild Grass

## Praise for this book

'Through the eyes of Rosa and her family, we experience in intimate detail the dramatic years of Nicaragua's triumphs and travail: the courageous struggle for freedom, the solidarity and idealism, the achievements and excitement about escape from suffering and submission, the cruel and bitter assault from abroad, defeat and betrayal, and still life goes on with its joys and sorrows, and the hope that never dies. A poignant, gripping, sensitive tale.'

*Noam Chomsky*

'The Sandinista Revolution to the Ortega Presidency in today's Nicaragua revealed through an epic family struggle. This book shows how Nicaraguan people felt and lived the revolution and continued to fight for its original values. A wonderful read.'

*Jenny Pearce,*
*Professor of Latin American Politics,*
*University of Bradford*

The protagonists speak for themselves and the author faithfully documents their accounts and also adds her own responses as a graphic artist through strong illustrations in which she interprets their voices and the reality of their lives. *Rosa of the Wild Grass* is very readable. I would heartily recommend it to anyone wanting to learn more about the contribution of women to the Sandinista revolution and how it impacted on their lives.'

*Marilyn Thomson,*
*co-director Central America Women's Network*

'This is a vivid and moving description of a small Latin American country's great struggle to free itself from crushing poverty and oppression. All told in the words of the people who have lived this history, it is as gripping and fascinating as Oscar Lewis's *La Vida*. Equally interesting is how the book recounts the aftermath of this period and how the Nicaraguans retain the spirit of what the revolution taught them, despite their continuing battle for survival.'

*Julie Christie, Actress*

# Rosa of the Wild Grass

## The Story of a Nicaraguan Family

Fiona Macintosh

Published by Practical Action Publishing Ltd in association with Latin America Bureau
The Schumacher Centre, Bourton on Dunsmore, Rugby, Warwickshire, CV23 9QZ, UK
www.practicalactionpublishing.org

Latin America Bureau,
Enfield House, Castle Street, Clun, Shropshire, SY7 8JU, UK
www.lab.org.uk

A catalogue record for this book is available from the British Library.
A catalogue record for this book has been requested from the
Library of Congress.

ISBN 978-1-90901-402-2 Hardback
ISBN 978-1-90901-403-9 Paperback
ISBN 978-1-90901-391-9 Library Ebook
ISBN 978-1-90901-392-6 Ebook

Citation: Macintosh, Fiona (2016) *Rosa of the Wild Grass: The Story of a Nicaraguan Family,*
Rugby, UK: Practical Action Publishing, <http://dx.doi.org/10.3362/9781909013919>

Since 1974, Practical Action Publishing has published and disseminated books and
information in support of international development work throughout the world.
Practical Action Publishing is a trading name of Practical Action Publishing Ltd
(Company Reg. No. 1159018), the wholly owned publishing company of
Practical Action. Practical Action Publishing trades only in support of its
parent charity objectives and any profits are covenanted back to Practical Action
(Charity Reg. No. 247257, Group VAT Registration No. 880 9924 76).

Latin America Bureau (Research and Action) Limited is a UK registered charity
(no. 1113039). Since 1977 LAB has been publishing books, news, analysis and
information about Latin America, reporting consistently from the perspective of
the region's poor, oppressed or marginalized communities and social movements.
In 2015 LAB entered into a publishing partnership with Practical Action Publishing.

Cover design by Fiona Macintosh
Printed by [printer, country]

FSC

# Contents

# Preface

I first met Rosa in Nicaragua in 1982. She worked as a plate maker in a print shop I used often to print the posters and education materials I designed. One day, talking over one of these print jobs, she invited me to her home in Managua to meet her family. So that next Saturday I went over on my motorbike to her *barrio*, a newly built neighbourhood, and asking around for Rosa was directed to a small wooden house.

Rosa introduced me to Rubén, her partner, and her son Darío and daughter Angélica. Rubén told me Rosa and he had built their home in a matter of days. Rosa was happy living there, despite having no electricity and starting her day by four in the morning to collect water from a communal tap.

I'd been there before to take photos. This was during an emergency to give shelter for hundreds of families left homeless after a week of torrential rains in May 1982. The photos show youthful volunteers working hard nailing walls, floors and roofs together in a collective effort so typical of those early years of the Sandinista revolution.

When I next saw Rosa she kindly invited me to her parents' home, which I was very pleased to accept. We took the bus from Managua, going south for some thirty kilometres to arrive in the hill town La Concha.

I'll always remember how her mother, María, warmly welcomed me. *'Esta es su casa'*, 'this is your house', and she meant it, always treating me like one of the family. But I don't think she knew just how much her home became a safe haven for me.

It was years later in 1987, after Rosa and I had become good friends, when this book was initiated by her and her mum. I was staying the weekend in La Concha and after breakfast María wrapped up some freshly baked *tortillas* in a cotton cloth, asking Rosa to take them to her sister, Flor. We left by the back door to take the short cut. Walking through the coffee grove, Rosa asked if I'd ever seen 'the view'. I knew La Concha but not much beyond, so, no, I hadn't seen 'the view'.

'Ah, you must,' Rosa said, and after visiting Flor, we set off along a dirt track out of town. When she turned off onto a narrow path, I followed to feel the breeze before reaching her under an immense tree, its roots clinging to an escarpment.

Dazzling green fields of pineapples and palms swept around the foothills that rose towards volcano Santiago. Its billowing immense white clouds trailed forever west. And far beyond, the capital shimmered against its background of Lake Managua, and further on still the land stretched towards the distant northern mountains. This was 'the view'.

Standing there with Rosa she pointed down below to a farmstead, saying she'd gone there during the insurrection. She said she went there to deliver a message for the Sandinistas. It was only then, after all these years, she started to tell me more about her involvement in the Sandinista revolution nine years ago. Our conversation that day was memorable, about her past and the present when we started talking about the Contra fighting in those northern mountains. At once those faraway mountains seemed all too close, the panorama being transformed with every word Rosa spoke.

'You've explained so much,' I told her and when I said, 'If you tell me again what you've said now, I could record', I knew Rosa understood. With her huge heart, wise head and a way with words and ideas, she knew she would tell an important story. She needed no encouragement before considering straight away what she wanted to say in this book.

'I'll start out talking about my brothers and sisters, and my dad farming,' she said, then decided to ask her mum if she'd like to contribute. We walked back to find María deftly separating grit from a pile of red beans. She said she'd be happy to join in.

Soon one recording was leading to another to become an all-engrossing and open-ended venture. I had no plan other than to follow their lead, listening to everything they said and only occasionally asking them to explain more. But I found myself wanting to respond to what they told me in the best way I could, by painting what became a series of raw-looking black and white illustrations. At the start all I was sure about was that mother and daughter occupied very distinct worlds that at the same time were closely interwoven. And I knew their voices would be an intimate portrayal of both themselves and their country.

I visited La Concha whenever I had a free weekend. In the cool of the late afternoons María and I would sit outside to talk and sometimes we'd decide to record. Rosa too was more able to talk there in La Concha, free of her daily responsibilities in Managua.

María's youngest daughter, Ana, still lived at the family home, which was basically one room with two bedrooms partitioned off. Ana slept in one with her children and husband and María slept in the other and set up folding cots for anyone visiting, like Rosa or the grandchildren, or me.

Most of Rosa's seven siblings still live locally. A whole day could be spent walking from one home to the other. Marcos lives next door to the family home, Flor seven blocks away, Dora on the other side of town and Guillermo, the eldest, in San Juan, the next town over. I would meet Rosa's youngest brother, Carlos, when he came home on visits; he had moved to the north of the country. Sergio too I got to know before he emigrated to Costa Rica.

La Concha is only an hour's bus ride from Managua, but to me it was of another world. The Catholic faith was as integral to the town's way of life as it was to Maria's. She drew a clear line between the good and bad that inhabited both this world and the next. She was concerned to explain how this spirit world lay firmly beneath the Church's authority and the benign rule of their past priest, Padre Ignacio.

Her life seemed defined by the town's continuum of annual religious festivities. She mentioned that during the Easter celebrations Padre Ignacio had borrowed uniforms and rifles from the local National Guard, the dictator's military police. This detail had me wondering about life under the Somoza dictatorship. It had been one of extreme inequalities but had lasted forty-three years. It must have depended on many forms of collusion including that between State and Church, to be always backed up by the brutal violence of Somoza's National Guard.

María was at ease talking about her life, until speaking about how the town's new priest was now running church affairs. She wouldn't say why, leaving it to Rosa to explain more about her mother's life and how it had been changed since the Sandinista revolution.

Rosa knew it was these changes that had brought me to Nicaragua and for this she trusted me. I'd told her I had worked in London as a graphic designer and was involved in helping Latin American refugee and human rights groups. Starting in 1964 and continuing throughout the 1970s there had been one military coup after another in southern Latin America, causing many to flee first from Brazil, then from Uruguay, Chile and Argentina. I told Rosa that when Nicaragua's dictatorship fell on July 19, 1979, it had been the best news I'd heard in a long time. I had wanted to see Nicaragua for myself, though I doubted that my graphic design skills would be in much demand. After the Sandinista revolution the country was in ruins. The war against dictator Somoza had caused fifty thousand deaths and three times that figure left wounded; with forty thousand orphans and half a million left homeless.

I thought at least I could visit, and in 1981 I crossed into Nicaragua from Costa Rica. Once I arrived in Managua I started showing my portfolio around to several of the new grassroots and labour organizations that had sprung up since the revolution. It turned out that there was in fact a great demand for my design skills. I was asked to design educational materials for the now free education being provided as part of the national reconstruction programme.

I made use of whatever materials were available. For the women's organization, AMNLAE, I painted Nicaragua's history from the perspective of women on stretches of gauze sheeting used on tobacco farms. It was a massive montage portraying life under the dictatorship, when life expectancy had been fifty-three years and one in twelve children had died at birth. Rosa's image could easily have been one of those women I portrayed onto the long roll of gauze. She had heart-felt reasons to support the revolution. For want of medical provision for the poor under the dictatorship, she and her sisters Flor and Dora each had a child with problems that could have been prevented. Rosa worked to ensure a mass turnout for the nationwide vaccination campaign in 1980 and was keen to see her own daughter vaccinated.

What I saw when I arrived was that no matter what the problem was, people were finding ingenious solutions. The country had taken charge of itself. Everyone was busy and everyone seemed to slot in, doing what was needed, using what post-war means were available. Rosa's brother Carlos had volunteered on the UNESCO-acclaimed adult literacy crusade. He was one of tens of thousands of students who effectively helped reduce adult illiteracy from fifty one percent to thirteen. This educational work was ongoing, and I too turned my skills to design some of the literacy manuals used on farms and in workplaces around the country. Seeing the methodology being refined was an education for me too. And on these design jobs I usually trained whoever was beside me. This handing on of skills was a necessity being duplicated everywhere and in all fields.

By 1983 I found permanent work with ATC, the farm workers' union, which supported the agrarian reform using the massive amount of land once owned by Somoza's family and close allies. One of my jobs was the union magazine. I'd be picked up at five in the morning by my journalist-farmer colleague to drive north and by nine he'd be interviewing women and men on the coffee and tobacco farms while I took photos. Seeing the agrarian reform in action was an eye-opener. The expectations of Rosa's father and brothers that the revolution would at last provide secure land and wages had been answered. The working and living conditions on these farms slowly improved. The ATC was ahead of other unions in recognizing the specific interests of women members, initiating forums that in turn influenced union policy.

The job broadened my perspective, but it was Rosa and her family who distilled for me the huge changes happening in the country. My relationship with them was open and for that reason was special. Being outspoken had held risks under the dictator and even after the victory in 1979. Fear fostered the well-honed tactics of survival: secrecy, collusion and denial.

Rosa had faced that fear and terror during the Sandinista insurrection, and having risked everything and survived, she gained a new confidence. She had moved on and had ambitions, not personal, but substantial. Rosa's directness came out of a hard-won victory and a conviction. She talked about the Sandinista revolution being like a release of fireworks, where everything surfaced. And when that energy coalesced she saw it building a better life with housing, schools, clinics, land for the landless and food made affordable for all. A great deal was achieved in those first four years and remarkably that made for growth in GDP, at a time when the rest of Central America was suffering a decline.

But that was to be the last growth for years. That day in 1987 when Rosa had taken me to see the view in La Concha, we'd talked about the fighting against the Contra in northern Nicaragua. The war had come to overshadow all that Rosa was working for and made telling this story imperative for her and for me.

Not long after I'd arrived in Nicaragua in 1981 Ronald Reagan was inaugurated as the US president, committed to 'rolling back' the Sandinista revolution. Some four-hundred million dollars was spent on CIA military training, intelligence and logistics to fuel a counter-revolutionary war. The CIA formed the initial Contra army from Somoza's exiled National Guardsmen, and bases were set up in Honduras. When travelling north I had asked my ATC colleague more about this insurgent army. He told me that while the leaders were National Guard officers, most of the foot soldiers were from the rural areas we were going to, and had no involvement in the revolution. He said they regarded the government land reform as coming from on high, and it was true that in these remote areas the reformed properties were often administered by outsiders who didn't always know what they were doing, so people didn't feel like beneficiaries. The peasants felt more beholden to their old landowners, who in their eyes had been replaced by another, larger landowner: the revolutionary State. Rosa had told me something similar: 'I had never thought there was anything but the rich being rich and the poor being poor, and that was life, just like Somoza and his family ruled the country and always would.'

Maybe in time this outlook would have changed but time wasn't given before the Contra began targeting the new farming cooperatives, schools and clinics.

Rosa knew there was a sliding scale between those who identified with the government's aims and those who didn't. At her print works Rosa came to accept that most of her work mates were looking in from the side-lines, guarded and fearful, a legacy she understood well that was rooted in the years of dictatorship. She could see her hopes draining away.

By 1988 Rosa had electricity in her home, she didn't have to go so far to collect water, and the clinic and the primary school where her daughter went were both well established, but her sense of urgency to record all she had worked for was real, because it was under threat.

That year I was working freelance again and went to the conflict zones in the Caribbean coast region and in the northern mountains to record what was happening for overseas charities. I was taking photos – a cattle shed sheltering some of the three-hundred thousand rural people displaced by the war; worn-looking women holding their babies; old men and children looking vacant after escaping a Contra attack. I still keep a melted medicine bottle that I picked out of the remains of a burned-down clinic. Economic and material damage was an enormous seventeen billion dollars.

The Contra war caused near thirty-one thousand deaths, leaving tens of thousands wounded and an estimated sixteen thousand children orphaned. The Reagan administration called this a 'low-intensity war'. It sowed terror and instability, wrecking an economy already battered by years of dictatorship and the violent insurrection. All this was in order to end 'the threat of a good example' for the poor of Latin America.

Ninety thousand men and women had served in the Sandinista Popular Army to fight against Reagan's Contra war. The war and the US blockade had sapped the country dry. By the end of 1988 I had ground to a stop. The daily headlines of another ambush, another funeral, another weeping mother draped over her son's coffin left me paralysed by grief and anger, and I too needed to escape.

I don't remember saying goodbye; it was all too painful. I left for Britain at the end of 1988.

I sat in my room in London listening to the recordings of María and Rosa. Hearing their voices, I couldn't settle. I was stuck in a dysfunctional state in Thatcher's Britain and was in no better frame of mind when I flew back to Nicaragua in 1990. I found Rosa not in good shape either. She kept asking again and again why so much suffering, for what? All she had worked for – a democratic, just and more open society – had been shut down. The war had deformed the country and again I recorded what she had to say. She explained that people had voted earlier that same year to change the government – out of desperation to end the war, to appease the US. Even some Sandinistas had voted for the US-backed UNO coalition and its candidate Violeta Chamorro.

This should have been a time to grieve, to draw breath, but no time was allowed before the new government started to slash public services, already cut by the cost of the war, and to dismantle state-owned enterprises, causing huge layoffs in addition to the tens of thousands of demobilized combatants on both sides. The war had caused trauma on a mass scale and now the social fabric was being shredded by neoliberal economic measures. How could anyone heal from trauma while such profound instability continued? Rosa, her family and her community, like others all over the country, were reeling.

How to survive, never mind address the trauma, became then the continuation of Rosa and her family's story. Many *barrios* like Rosa's subsisted out of necessity, experience and sheer endurance. Rosa told me in 1994 she was now working together with other women in her *barrio* on a soya project to feed poor mothers and children, the hungry fallout of the neoliberal 'machine'. The *barrio* project was supported by overseas aid and Rosa was rooting for what mattered to her and those around her. She and her women friends were recovering by being together, doing what they needed for themselves. What they wanted for their community was more than survival. They were talking about something they had never discussed before – that their own self-worth and their capacity as community workers were one and the same. Despite her personal and family difficulties, Rosa had come into her own. Over the years she became an excellent cook and herbalist who enthused others. She and her friends had grown into an informal network of nutritionists and social workers. Rosa talked about their work spreading like 'wild grass', without boundaries or borders.

But in her *barrio* and in Rosa's own life as well, the fallout continued. She again had to face terror and in surviving for the second time she didn't look outwards to change the world but, holding onto her wild grass seeds, took the calmer path to La Concha. She needed to be closer to her family. She had gone through huge changes and in 2008 explained to me how she felt her family in La Concha was her bedrock, wondering if she would be still alive without them. It was only natural, she said, for all of them to now become part of the book. I agreed and began to record those keen to join in. As each one told his or her own story – tales of marital breakdown and migration, of hardships and hopes – they brought alive their kindred spirit, and their strength and determination to survive. Three generations speak in this book, each one revealing the costs of the disproportionate extremes of wealth and poverty in this second-poorest country in Latin America.

On my last visit five years later, in 2013, I accompanied Rosa taking her two grandsons to the local school. She was caring for them just like her mother had helped her with her children and like her grandmother had done before that.

When we went through the manuscript together and corrected a few points, Rosa was clear that we had reached the end; she was content in herself and content with the book.

The last day in La Concha, Rosa took me to see her sister Dora. All who could make the gathering had come and we sat together chatting under the orange trees in the garden. They told me they had decided it would be wiser for their names and some locations to be changed. They didn't want to invite the curious or cause upset and we had a good laugh coming up with pseudonyms. There was never going to be a time to leave. I had to make myself go. I thanked them all and left on the bus for Managua.

All that the family told me I have translated and the events they describe are all true. The significance of their experiences rests within the larger story of Nicaragua's history.

I am extremely grateful to Judy Butler for her continued loyal support and encouragement over this long journey of twenty-seven years, throughout which she was living in Nicaragua. In addition to her careful and constructive edit of the final manuscript, she supplied me with the detailed factual and chronological background I needed, both in response to my questions and through the columns of Nicaragua's analytical journal, *Envío*, whose English edition she edits.

*Fiona Macintosh*

*Rosa's family tree*

## Cast of characters

**Alfonso,** Husband of Rosa's sister Dora.

**Allan,** Laura's son and Rosa's grandson.

**Ana**, Rosa's younger sister, lives in the family home in La Concha with her partner, Lucho, and five children.

**Angélica**, Rosa and Rubén's daughter, a policewoman, lives in La Concha and is mother of Richie and Iván.

**Antonio**, Rosa's boss at her print works.

**Arnoldo Alemán**, Mayor of Managua, 1990–95, and President of Nicaragua 1997–2002.

**Blanca,** Carlos's wife and Rosa's sister-in-law.

**Brígida**, Rosa's great-aunt on her mother's side.

**Cabrera family**, in Managua, Rosa works for them as a maid

**Carlos**, Rosa's youngest brother, an agronomist-teacher, lives in northern Nicaragua with his wife Blanca and three children.

**Cecilia**, Rosa first visits in 1988, and introduces to the *barrio* project, SoyaNica, in 1991.

**Clara**, Rosa's *barrio* friend in Managua.

**Claudia**, daughter of Doña Ester.

**Darío**, Rosa and Rubén's son.

**David**, Rosa's first boyfriend and Laura's father.

**Domingo**, a judge and landowner and Rosa's distant cousin on her mother's side.

**Dora**, Rosa's older sister, a seamstress, lives in La Concha, is married to Alfonso, and is mother of Mauricio and Pilar.

**Emilio**, Sara's boyfriend, a peasant, lives in La Concha.

**Ernesto**, María's brother and Rosa's uncle.

**Esmeralda**, neighbour of María, Rosa's mum, is married to Don Victor.

(Doña) **Ester**, herbalist in La Concha.

**Evita**, Flor's daughter and Rosa's niece.

(Don) **Federico**, Sandinista activist. He and his wife, Inés, employ Rosa in the late 1970s in Managua.

**Flor**, Rosa's younger sister, an artisan, lives in La Concha with husband Enrique and children Hector, Evita and Florcita.

**Frida**, union secretary at the print works where Rosa works.

**Gabriel**, Laura's youngest son and Rosa's grandson.

(Dr) **García**, Rosa works for him as a maid in Managua.

**Guillermo**, Rosa's eldest brother, a builder, lives in San Juan, the next town to La Concha, and is father of Myrna.

**Heraldo**, Laura's husband and Rosa's son-in-law. is an accountant in Managua, and lives in La Concha.

(Padre) **Ignacio**, Parish priest in La Concha during María's lifetime.

**Inés**, Sandinista activist. She and her husband Federico employ Rosa in the late 1970s.

**Iván**, Angélica and Mateo's son, Rosa's grandson.

**Laura**, Rosa and David's daughter. Employed by agricultural co-op bank in La Concha, where she lives with husband Heraldo and sons Allan and Gabriel.

**Leda**, Rosa's *barrio* friend in Managua.

**Marcos**, Rosa's older brother, agricultural worker and builder in La Concha, and father of two daughters.

**María**, lives in La Concha and is mother of Guillermo, Sergio, Dora, Marcos, Rosa, Flor, Ana and Carlos.

**Mateo**, married Angélica, is father of Iván, and lives in Managua.

**(Padre) Marlon**, La Concha's priest, murdered August 2011

**Mauricio**, Dora's son and Rosa's nephew.

**Myrna**, Guillermo's daughter and Rosa's niece.

**Lucho**, partner of Ana, Rosa's sister, a peasant farmer in La Concha.

(Sister) **Lupita**, coordinator of the community project SoyaNica in Rosa's *barrio* in Managua.

**Daniel Ortega**, FSLN President, 1985-1990, and again in 2007, incumbent (2015).

**Oscar**, Rosa's workmate at her print works, whose son Tomás is killed in a Contra ambush.

**Paco**, married to Evita. Evita is Flor's daughter and Rosa's niece.

**Pilar**, Dora's daughter and Rosa's niece.

**Ramón**, Rosa has known him since he was a child in her Managua *barrio*.

**René**, Rosa's Sandinista friend killed in the 1979 FSLN insurrection.

**Richie,** Angélica and Mickey's son, and Rosa's grandson.

**Rigoberta**, Rosa's close *barrio* friend in Managua.

**Rita**, mother-in-law of Laura, Rosa's daughter, and lives in Managua.

**Rubén**, Rosa's partner and father of Angélica and Darío.

**José María Salas**, landowner in La Concha.

**Sara**, Rosa's adopted daughter.

**Sarah**, an American woman Rosa works for as a maid and nanny.

**Sergio**, Rosa's older brother, plumber and builder, married with three children; he and his family emigrate to Costa Rica.

**Susana**, Rosa's close Sandinista friend.

**Tina**, Rosa's aunt on her father's side, who lives in Managua.

**Ernesto Tórrez**, a community committee organizer in Rosa's *barrio* in Managua.

**Velázquez family**, Rosa works for them as a maid.

(Don) **Valerio**, the father of Rosa's partner, Rubén

(Don) **Victor**, neighbour and distant relative to Rosa's mum, María.

(Doña) **Violeta**, UNO President from 1990 to 1997.

**William**, husband of Pilar, who is Dora's daughter and Rosa's niece.

# 1 Between you and me

*It is 1987, some eight years since the bloody insurrection and overthrow of the Somoza dictatorship. The government, confirmed by elections in 1984, is formed by the FSLN, the Sandinistas. Rosa is now thirty-six, and María, her mother, in her late fifties.*

## Rosa

Did you hear Marcos banging on the door last night? What a racket: *'Madre mía,* let me in! Son of a bitch, this is my bloody house!'

Bring your coffee, we can talk under the tree. His mind gets working when he's drunk, especially when I'm home. He's always been jealous of me. He says I've no right to be interfering, he's the one in charge. He knows I've told Mum to sell the small-holding outside town and enjoy the money. She should; Mum has worked all her life and should be taking it easy. Even now she won't take a weekend off. For her, life is work. If she sold now it would avoid a lot of bother later on. The trouble is Dad told Marcos he was to look after the household affairs once he passed away, and now Marcos is saying this isn't the time to sell, that there isn't the market and Mum should go on selling the oranges and mandarins. He's right in that there's not much demand for land since the agrarian reform. But I know what my brother is really up to: he's banking on inheriting the land after Mum dies.

His drinking is out of hand. I don't like it. I only ever saw Dad drunk once or twice. There was none of this shouting, waking the ghosts. If ever Dad had a drink on him, he'd quietly ask Mum to hang up the hammock and he'd take a nap, that was all. The

1

*'Madre mía, let me in!'*

*guaro* was brewed only for men to relax after a hard day's work, to sit out and have a chat.

When passing Los Cocos on the bus up here, the woman sitting beside me told me she'd gone to see the herbalist in Los Cocos about her boy. She said he was sleeping rough, out of his mind on drink, but after she gave him the herbal remedy it was as if he became brand new. Marcos could do with a dose of that.

No, you don't want to be near him when he's on one of his binges. He'll be gone for days after he's brought in the harvest. He's in a cooperative now. He's never left La Concha.

\* \* \*

It was us girls who left to go to the city to earn some cash. I left when I was thirteen. We weren't that poor but money was always tight. That was 1964, when I finished at the local primary school

2

in La Concha, I'd attended with my five brothers and sisters. The older ones had already left when I started.

I did pretty well at school and when I was twelve the school held a small assembly. In those days they didn't have this Sash of Excellence for the best student but the school director told me, 'Rosa, you've always been very studious and had top marks. You must go on with your schooling; there's a bright future ahead of you.' She said I should tell my mum and dad to register me for high school.

I felt so proud telling Dad, 'The director said I'll have a bright future if I go on to high school. She said there'd be no cost other than the uniform and school materials.'

Dad said, 'Well, that's good to hear, but you've finished school now.' He wouldn't listen. 'No Rosa. It's the boys who need an education. They're going to have the responsibilities of wife and family. When you find a good man, he'll keep you.'

I didn't understand so went to Mum. 'Dad says I can't go on to high school. What am I supposed to do?'

'Now there's plenty to get on with: the coffee picking and you can go and help plant the corn.'

'But I don't want this. I'm going to find some other work.'

In the end I was stuck at home doing all the household chores.

My friends all knew what had happened. Terri, who I knew from church, kept saying to me, 'Maybe your dad will change his mind.'

'If he hasn't in a year, he's not going to now. You know what he's like. I'll look for a job.'

I thought that would at least be better than washing and cooking at home; I'd be earning. It was normal for girls like me to go to the city for work. You'd hear that kind of thing on the bus. 'Juanita, she's left, got a cleaning job in Managua, and her sister, she's with a big coffee family.'

So I asked Terri to keep an ear out. 'Whatever you find tell me – any job … like cleaning.' She was a year older than me and I saw her as very grown up. She went to Managua a lot to visit her relatives.

A week later she came to find me. 'Listen, my cousin needs someone to be with her. I think it won't be more than keeping her company and the flat is really small.' Her cousin had just got married but the husband was never home so the young bride was lonely and her mum felt she needed someone to be with her.

'Ideal. I'll go.'

In my head I was already on my way when I told Mum. I asked Terri to come too, to put Mum's mind to rest. But she said a lot more. She said, 'Rosa wants to go because she wants to study.'

'But how do you know they'll let Rosa out to go to school?'

'I'll find out,' I said.

In the end Mum gave in. 'Well, I'll need to know who these people are.'

Dad was upset too, but that next Sunday I was on the bus to Managua with my bag. Mum came with me.

The wife's name was Pata. She was only a few years older than me and Terri was right, there was little to do other than wash the dishes and clothes. The only thing was, back home we had an earth floor so mopping the tiled floor was all new to me. I broke a crystal vase and a couple of plates and Pata's mum gave me a terrible time for that. I began wondering if I'd made a big mistake and should go home. But when I was paid for the first time, I felt thirty *córdobas* was a fortune and I stayed on.

But thirty *córdobas* wasn't enough to pay for evening classes and after eight months had rolled by I heard of another position. A maid I often met at the corner shop told me a woman in her block was looking for a maid from out of town. 'Why not try?

4

Doña Nuevia wants a live-in maid, someone reliable.' When she said the pay was sixty *córdobas,* I said, 'That's me.'

Pata was now pregnant and her mum wanted an older maid for her, so all round my leaving was fine.

Doña Nuevia obviously wanted more for her sixty *córdobas* than just cleaning. She wanted me babysitting all the time. At least I was now saving and when I had enough to enrol in school I asked Doña Nuevia for time off, but she said, 'My dear, that's exactly why I need you, to allow me to go to night classes, and the other evenings I need you here for when I have visitors.'

It took two years before I found a day job with Angela and her husband in Managua. And my Aunty Tina, one of my Dad's sisters, offered to let me move in with her and her daughter. For me Tina was like a second mum; she was a real support.

At last I was going to the Pan Americana School in the Monseñor Lezcano *barrio.* I went there for two years and passed all my exams.

Then Tina suggested I go to technical college. University wasn't on the cards but I wanted to learn a skill so I applied to a college near Ciudad Jardín to learn typing and bookkeeping. The classes ran from six to eight in the evenings. I had this voice in my head saying, 'Stick with it, keep going. In the end you'll have a proper job and proper money,' but at the same time I knew the money I was spending on college was needed back home.

Once I qualified, I went looking for secretarial or bookkeeping jobs. I looked everywhere, even in the Eastern Market, but it was 1970 so businesses were shutting down and no investment was happening in the country. All that effort ended up with me being no better off. I was stuck in my maid's job.

\* \* \*

It was then I met David. He used to come by the house where I was working, selling bread every day. He asked me where I was from and when I told him La Concha he said he was from there too. He knew of my dad and mum and also Aunty Tina. And soon as he knew I was sleeping over at Tina's, he began dropping in to see me there. I was only eighteen, way too young and all wrapped up in myself. All I knew about a man and a woman was what Mum had said, which was, 'Give one good reason why a man should hold a woman's hand.' Truly. I never saw Mum and Dad openly show affection. And they didn't know about David. No, in those days no one talked about contraceptives, but they weren't available anyway. Birth control wasn't something anybody talked about, much less sex. When I got pregnant I kept it private, secret, and I felt terrible.

When slowly the bump began to appear, Tina asked me directly and I just broke down in tears and told her. She was really shocked. She thought I'd have had more sense. She was kind though. I asked her if she would tell Mum for me, ha, and of course when she told them, Mum got upset and Dad was furious with Tina for allowing this to happen under her roof.

I felt so bad I asked the woman I worked for, Angela, if I could stay at their place. And she said yes. She made me feel at home. I'll always be grateful to her. She's a nurse and that was a real blessing; she understood what I was going through.

For the duration of my pregnancy I hardly ever went out, fearing I'd see Tina, and I hardly saw David. He was too macho. Whenever I'd gone anywhere with him he wouldn't let me wear makeup, wanting me to look like a nun in a long skirt, and he'd introduce me to his friends as his woman.

I'd told him, 'No, I'm not your woman. I'm Rosa and I'm used to working, going out, looking smart, and I've got friends who want to see me and I want to see them.' He didn't even like me seeing my pals from college. I couldn't take how he tried to control me and after six months my love for him was over. Way before Laura was born we'd parted company. I was nineteen when I had Laura.

Angela and her husband were very kind. Angela kept sending me for prenatal check-ups at the hospital. I gave birth there and only Angela was with me. Laura's birth changed everything.

David, though, wasn't willing to accept our separation. He came to Angela's to try and persuade me to go back. I told him, 'It was hard enough giving birth. Please, I don't need any more grief.' He just wouldn't take no for an answer. 'Come on, we can make a go of this,' he'd insist.

'How can we if I'm not the person you want me to be? I am Rosa, and I know it won't work. Laura and I are going to be fine so don't worry.' He kept turning up on the door step until at last I heard he had another girlfriend. What a relief when he stopped coming.

* * *

All this time I hadn't been home. I knew Mum was worried and she must have talked Dad around because Tina came to tell me I should go home with Laura. But when I did, Dad gave me such a telling off, letting me know exactly what he thought, saying I should be in a proper relationship and married. It was my brother Sergio who came to my rescue. He said David was a bully and a drunk, which wasn't true. David had no bad habits like drinking, but I wasn't going to argue.

Despite Mum and Dad being annoyed, they didn't reject me and I saw Mum loved Laura. They accepted her into the home. Once Laura was a toddler she went to stay with them. Mum saw to it that she went to school, gave her the security she needed, and pushed her in her studies. I simply wasn't in a position to do that. It was for the best. It's only to be expected she grew up to

7

feel close to her granny, closer maybe than to me, and yes, that has made me sad. I had no choice but to work and make sure Laura had what she needed.

Laura has always been top of her class. She's sixteen now. I can see how she holds her own. She's grown into a bright, mature young woman. I could depend on Mum. My sister Ana wouldn't have bothered herself. Ana doesn't see the importance of education. She still lives at home with Mum and her family. What really got my goat was how she'd use Laura to do her washing and at the same time pretend she bought Laura her clothes. When I found out I told Laura, 'It's only right you respect your Aunty Ana. But Laura, I'm your mother and I'm the one who pays for everything you need. If ever I didn't, you'd be the first to know.' I made sure I said this in Ana's hearing and then I told Ana that Laura wasn't her maid. I'll never forget that and I doubt she has.

It was Mum who wanted the best for Laura and that was to learn. Mum treasured education. I'd often heard her say so. I remember when I was small, it was at the end of Mum's class and Dad came in and for some reason I asked him if he could read and he said he wished he could and, there and then, Mum sat down beside him with her books and started to teach him. Why Dad didn't send me to high school was because money was always tight. They had to sacrifice a lot to see Carlos and Sergio go to college. And Dora too; she trained to be a seamstress.

Dora paid them back soon as she could, after she set up the sewing cooperative. That was a real success for her. She set it up with other women in La Concha. That was soon after the Sandinistas came into power in 1979.

Too bad Dora hasn't the same get-up-and-go regarding Alfonso. He thinks I give Dora ideas but he's got no worries there. Before she married him I tried telling her, but she insisted, 'If I don't marry now, when will I?'

'It's not when you marry, it's who you marry that's important.'

He's another drunk, like Marcos.

She had a choice and she must have known what she was letting herself in for. Her marriage hadn't been arranged like in my parents' time. Then it would have been. Yes, my grandparents arranged for Mum and Dad to marry. That was the custom then. I suppose my grandparents must have thought they'd make a good couple. They'd have said, 'María makes fine *tortillas*, nothing is too much of a chore for her, and Roberto is a hard-working and honest man.' Then Mum was told to go and see the priest, and two weeks later she and Dad walked down the aisle. That's what Mum told me. But look, they were well suited. They must have been to stay married for fifty years.

In those days you had to respect your parents. If you didn't, you could be cut off. My Sunday school teacher, Lucía, a tall elegant lady, looked almost like the Virgin Mary herself. The problem was her dad; he was too strict with her. He said he was waiting for the right man for her and that's why she was still single at the age of twenty-nine. Then one day a farmhand turned up to pick coffee. I heard people in church saying, 'Lucía's talking to that peasant. He must have sprinkled that magic potion *Sontin* by her window.' Folk thought he'd put a spell on her. But soon as her dad got wind of this he sent the man packing.

No one imagined Lucía would run away. This was a mortal sin for the family. For months no one saw her parents. They kept behind closed doors. And no one saw Lucía, not for another year until after she had her baby.

Her father gave her a smallholding outside La Concha where she still lives with her man. He gave the land to save face, but she was cut off and never seen in church again. She only appeared in town to sell *tortillas*. All that happened when I was a small girl.

## Rosa's mum, María

Maybe it was because I was their only girl, and clever, that my parents decided to send me to the religious school in the next town. On the Monday morning my father would take me there on his horse, and come and fetch me on the next Saturday.

I stayed with an aunt and she cooked me my meals. We'd bring her rice, beans, cassava, coffee, *pinolillo* and oranges so she never went short. I stayed there until I was fourteen years old and when I left I was able to teach.

I went to teach on two farms outside La Concha, a fair distance to walk but I always felt it was worthwhile. The children's parents were very appreciative, always giving me little presents for helping their children, and they had next to nothing themselves.

I taught the children arithmetic, the alphabet and how to write in script and pronounce words up to three syllables. I taught at these two farms until I married Roberto. Then I thought I could do the same from home for the children in La Concha. I taught twenty little children and my own children joined the classes too. I taught in the shade on the patio and when it rained we moved indoors. After a year with me the children were ready to enrol at the local primary and they always went up one class, so that tells you they learned something! Only the other day a woman asked if I'd consider tutoring her boy. I think he'd be better going to the new nursery and told her so, but isn't that nice? I'm still thought of as the teacher after all these years.

I was never properly trained. Padre Ignacio actually came to enquire if I'd consider going to teacher training college in Masaya for the proper qualification. I wanted nothing better but mother said looking after my children would be too much for her. Padre Ignacio was obviously very interested in me going though, because he visited again and this time with the head of the college, but no, my mother would not change her mind. He must have been determined, coming twice especially to talk to her, but I couldn't take up his offer and in the end I had to give up teaching. This was after I had my fifth baby. Mother could no longer cope and said I had to stop teaching.

Instead we thought I could go twice a week to sell fruit in the city and mother said she could manage to mind the children for those days. I went with two friends of mine. We hired a cart to take us as far as the train station in San Marcos to catch the five o'clock train and there paid a lad to lift our baskets onto the wagon. The train journey was beautiful. We'd pass Masatepe, Caterina, Niquinohomo then go on to Masaya and Sábana Grande and at each stop more market women got on. We'd arrive in Managua at seven o'clock. The Eastern Market was next to the station and we'd have our stalls set out with sweet and bitter oranges, lemons, gourds and bananas before the shoppers arrived. It's the busiest, noisiest place in the world; everyone came, the poorest and the richest with their servants. With what I made I bought what we needed: rice and cheese, whatever we didn't grow.

Then I went back on the afternoon train. Everything could be found in the Eastern Market but we could grow enough not to go hungry. My father and uncles worked the land. Mother and I were only needed in the fields for the planting and harvest time. Before the planting we went to hang streamers from the trees to scare off the birds, and the men nailed straw crosses scented with lemon at the four corners of the field. The men urinated there too, but nothing scared away the monkeys, those little bandits.

11

And for pests from farther away, that took a special boy. We would ask family friends who had such a boy. He'd been born in his placenta so was gifted. He knew what to do: he walked naked across our field in a way to make the sign of the cross. Most years this worked and we grew more than we needed. Only once did we lose the harvest. We could see the insects flying in and like a cloud they rained down onto the corn fields. Everyone came

*He walked naked across our field in a way to make the sign of the cross*

rushing out with pots and pans, we were banging madly, making such a din, but those insects must have been deaf. Chomp, chomp, chomp, they ate and ate until not a stalk was left. There was nothing we could do. That was a hard year. We had little to eat. Everyone had to get by helping each other with what they had. Most years though, we had enough to eat.

The shops you see today in La Concha didn't exist then. The village was smaller and quieter and much more shaded in those days by great tall trees. When we had those trees it was much cooler. The orange and mandarin trees are smaller and grown only to serve us.

In La Concha everyone knew each other and the whole town would come together for the Saints' Days. We'd celebrate each one with a *fiesta* and Holy Week was the most special of all. On the Easter Monday our family went to the Río Conquista. We all went: my parents, grandparents, aunts and uncles, and the small ones went in the cart. We set off early in the morning when it was fresh to spend the whole day beside the river.

Yes, that was how we lived. We cared for one another and life was like that. I lived with my parents; I lived with them until they departed from this world.

When father was an old man he took ill. We went to Jinotepe to find the doctor and he came in his car. But it was no use. Four days later father passed away. He had worked all his life.

Then four years later mother passed away. Those were sad times. Mother has been gone now thirty years. I still miss her. She took care of us all.

\* \* \*

Before I married Roberto I asked his parents if they would accept me going on living with my parents and for Roberto to move in with us. They knew I was their only girl and I explained how mother needed me and wanted my company, and that I cooked father's supper every day and helped with the washing and ironing. I told them how mother liked to wear a fresh dress every day and father liked his shirt starched for Sunday Mass. For all of this they agreed with me that I did not have to move into their home.

This way we helped each other. Mother had lost almost all of her other children, twelve of them. They all died very young, some from fevers, others from diarrhoea. Only my brother Ernesto and I remained. When mother lost her last baby she had to sell her store of beans to pay the doctor. That was why mother wanted me with her and she wanted my children around her too. This is where we have always lived, and after I married Roberto, father and Ernesto and my oldest boy Guillermo built the large room where I taught.

Ernesto was a builder by trade and for a time he did very well. He built his own home and other houses in La Concha. Sadly it was the drink that changed his fortune. Mother tried many ways to stop him; she pleaded with him and punished him but he couldn't stop. He lost everything; he even sold the land he had inherited. It was then mother said, 'Ernesto's never going to sort himself out.' He'd inherited his land from Brígida, my mother's sister.

That was why mother loved so much having my children with her. She was always concerned for them. She taught me all the remedies she knew for fevers and diarrhoea and they worked well. When my second boy Sergio was small he was often poorly and came down once with stomach heat. Mother gave him milk of magnesium mixed with a few drops of lemon and liquor. She then bathed him with rue, basil, chili leaves and wild aloe, some *madroño* leaves, alcohol and a little of his urine. And after that I wrapped him up and he went to sleep. For three days I gave him these baths until he was better.

14

Mother showed me how to control fevers using the water from boiling leaves from the flamboyant tree; that acts as a laxative too. And *guava* leaves too can help with diarrhoea. So can cassava. Tie a teaspoon of cassava in a cotton bag and boil it in water until it is thick, thick. Maybe this kills the parasites, I don't know. But if you have bleeding as well, that'll be an intestinal illness and then it's advisable to see a doctor. Mother gave me many remedies and showed me how to draw out air from beneath the skin. Take a candle to heat air inside a glass and then quickly place it on the affected area and that will pull the air right out and stop the muscle cramping or quivering.

You know to take care your baby doesn't see a drunk? If he looks into the baby's eyes that can cause a fever; the alcohol heat can penetrate. Yes, and take care when pregnant yourself with your first baby not to look any baby in the eyes. That too can cause your unborn baby a fever. Not always though; my first pregnancy was fine even after a friend asked me to see her new babe.

If I couldn't find a cure I would turn to Doña Ester. She lived near here, down the road. I took Sergio to her when I couldn't bring down his fever. She has a special way of massaging, then she held him upside down to smack the soles of his feet and pressed her thumb into the top of his mouth and this way the fever fell out. Doña Ester was a very gifted healer. She lived in the green house behind the palms with her husband and her daughter Claudia. You never saw her out on the street; she kept to herself. She had mystical powers.

Claudia came to me first when Doña Ester passed away. I had taught Claudia when she was little. I asked her in for a cup of coffee. She was always a good girl and I think she may have her mother's gift. I was very taken by how calm she was. She told me that the night before she had heard her mother praying to the saints, as she always did. Her mother kept the images of Peter, Paul, Luke and John on her dressing table. Then later on she'd heard her mother call her, 'Claudia, please bring me a glass of water', and when Claudia came through to her room, she found her mother dead. Claudia said nothing had been wrong with her mother, that it was a mystery why she had died.

Poor girl, all alone and she managed to dress her mother's corpse, dear me. You see, at the time her father was away working. She seemed so composed telling me this. I asked her how she was coping and she said, 'Mother told me not to be upset when she passed away. I'm only doing what she told me to do.' Perhaps she didn't feel that alone because she said she felt her mother's presence in the house.

Since Doña Ester departed I've been going to the new health centre set up by the Sandinista government. They charge very little, only for the medicines. I think their doctor and the nurse are good. If they don't have the medicines in stock, the state pharmacy in San Marcos usually does and one of my children will go pick it up. They are happy to help. Most of my children live nearby. Only Rosa and Carlos live far away. Carlos, my youngest, lives near Matagalpa. He's twenty-five years old. He's a teacher with a good job there. And Rosa, she lives in Managua.

Sergio lives nearby. He's a plumber by trade and people with money hire him to install their toilets. He's in the midst of building his own home. It will have three rooms with proper walls and he's laying a concrete floor. His plantains have given him a good return this year. He said he harvested three thousand. He's doing well.

His training to become a plumber cost us a lot. It was the price of his technical books that had me turn to my cousin, Domingo, for a loan. Thankfully we were able to pay him back with that year's coffee and orange harvest. Unfortunately though, Sergio's graduation forced us to turn to Domingo again. He advised us to sell him part of our holding.

After paying for Sergio's shoes and gown, all we had left was enough to paint the big room and buy a new cooking pot.

## Rosa

Mum and Dad had to sell part of our holding, but even after that they were still owing money to Domingo. Dad only got Domingo off his back when he found work with the state water utility, when they came to install water in La Concha. That gave him two years' paid work and Mum made some extra selling fruit juice to the workmen.

Domingo was the son of my granny's sister on Mum's side of the family. He was her only son and she saw to it that he had a proper university education. He was a man of preparation and became a judge and made good use of his money. Folk would go to him if they had a health problem, food shortage or needed a grant for education. He'd lend them the money. 'Yes, come to me if you need cash for your seeds and fertilizer.' And after the harvest was sold the farmers paid him. But before sowing time Domingo would be back on their shoulder, like a spider they could never brush off.

At his interest rates, Domingo only had to bide his time until a poor harvest, wait till the farmers couldn't pay and then he'd have them turfed off their land. That was how he gained more and more until he had an enormous amount of land.

Because we were a big family we were always hard up, so Mum was forced to go to him. I know she felt humiliated by him and when they couldn't pay back in time, Dad had to work for him

17

*He'd have them turfed off their land*

for nothing. I think we only held on to what's left of the holding because his mother had words with Domingo.

What a misery he was. Domingo had diabetes and that was why he had his foot amputated. He ended his days in a wheel-chair. One of his daughters took him in to live with her in Masaya and his big farm was left to go wild and his house is now a shell. He died five years after his mother passed away. A son-in-law from Chile took over but he can't be interested; he's an intellectual. He just leaves the place for some labourers to pick the fruit and coffee.

Domingo might have had a close family had he not been so arrogant. After Mum's aunt died we stopped visiting. He was a man who sinned, like many another. What he did was no different from any other landowner. This was how small farmers lost the little they had and this was only ended by the Sandinistas.

After the revolution the farm workers' union gave many of the landless farmers work on lands the Sandinista government had confiscated. The land was taken from those landowners who had sided with the dictator. Many farmers in La Concha could have reclaimed their old lands, but I suppose it was easier for them to join the newly formed farming cooperatives like Dad and Marcos did. The peasants in La Concha, they're unsure of themselves, they think these landowners will be back one day and send them packing. Dad, though, was never in any doubt. He was one of the first in La Concha to join the farming union. He said, 'No land-owner will ever boss me about again, demanding I work all hours and for a pittance.'

Every year he left us for a couple of months to go and work on the cotton harvest to make some ready cash. Sometimes one of my brothers went with him. At three in the morning he said the bell rang for everyone to get up and out in the fields and they had no breakfast until nine when they ate some rice and beans. He said many had no other life but that, working all year round moving from farm to farm, from harvest to harvest. He and my brother slept together in a big bunk in a huge shed along with hundreds of other men, women and children. Whole families had one bunk. There were no facilities. It was filthy, Dad said, rats running about everywhere. He told us a baby died from a fever and there was nothing they could do, the baby just died. It was this and much more that made Dad the man he was and he stood up for his beliefs.

* * *

I'd say most folk in La Concha have never supported the Sandinistas, not like they do in León, Estelí or Matagalpa. Last

19

Sunday I went with Mum to Mass and to hear what that priest was preaching. Praying for the salvation of the Sandinistas from damnation, would you believe it? People wouldn't dare question him, no, no. They'd give their last and best hen and pig for a blessing from the archbishop. Their faith runs deep, through the generations. It's deep and rooted.

I've always gone to Mass, since I was a baby. Sunday Mass was the family entertainment! I still go to Mass in Managua, though my church there is a Popular Church. I like what my priest says about life is to be made better here, in this life, not in the next. He asks why would Christ want us going about with heads bowed down. He says Christ wants us to live with dignity. And if we have to defend

*Their faith runs deep, through the generations*

that dignity then we have to. If we're being attacked, which we are, then Christ would say, 'Protect yourself', wouldn't he?

I know Mum doesn't like me talking like this. She refuses to see how manipulative their new priest in La Concha is. No, and she won't hear a word spoken against the archbishop, about how he twists the Christian message for justice and fairness.

She's very devoted. Oh, when Ana suggested after thirty years Mum needn't hold a memorial for her parents, she was most put out. 'Where's your sense of respect? How would your grandparents feel coming home to no shrine, no flowers, no food?' And Carlos too, she gave him a right ticking off. She told him she'd make the arrangements herself to have his children baptized. They're Carlos's children but she won't accept that he wants to wait until they're old enough to make up their own minds.

Dad was never devout in the way Mum is but he had cause to respect the Saints' Days. He'd never work on Ascension Day. He'd not touch his machete, no, not since a friend of his had told him he'd wanted to work on that day and just as he was tying his ox to the plough he heard, 'Today no, tomorrow yes.' And the only other living creature there was his ox. So Dad took that to heart.

Maybe not Saints' Days, but I've always been mindful of what I know are warnings, or what you call premonitions. I had a warning, or more I'd say a nightmare, when I had Laura with me; she was only eight months at the time. I'd moved from Angela's to work for an American family in Managua. In my nightmare I was in their flat and the whole place began trembling. Everything started to break up and I was holding onto Laura but then the floor split open under me and Laura fell from my arms, down through the crack and I couldn't do a thing to save her. I woke up in total panic and hugged Laura tight.

That day Mum came to visit me. She wanted to know if I'd be home for Christmas and I told her I would, but then I thought that, as she was there, she could take Laura back home with her, which she was happy to do. I gave her my powdered milk and off they went. I don't know why, maybe it was the dream, but I felt she should be with Mum.

It was that very next night the earthquake struck Managua. This was December 23, 1972. The earthquake destroyed the city. It was a disaster too huge to imagine. We were living on the ground floor. It was as if we were inside a volcano with everything falling about us. The apartment collapsed like a fan folding in on itself.

I don't know how we got out but their little girl was left trapped inside. Her father was like a crazed man and got hold of a piece of the wall and lifted it like it was a sheet of cardboard. He had this superhuman strength and there was his girl. Her cot sides had folded in just enough so she wasn't crushed. She'd been hit by stones and glass and had dust up her nose, but incredibly her Dad saved her. Yes, she survived.

And it was my dream, my nightmare that had saved Laura.

The American family, they wanted to leave as soon as they could and Sarah, the wife, asked if I would go with them, but of course I needed to be with Laura so I came home to La Concha. The only work I could find was picking coffee and the pay was a pittance. That next year was tough. Four in the morning I was up and had to walk several kilometres to the farm. It was thirsty, hungry work and those insects, they bit me raw. I could never pick enough coffee, only a quarter of what anyone else did so my earnings were barely enough to feed Laura. I'd have been bare-foot but for my friends.

Then one afternoon I came home to find Sarah sitting on the patio. I was so happy to see her. She'd come especially to find me

22

and I was more than pleased when she asked if I'd work for them again. Right there and then I packed and Laura and I went to their new home in Catarina.

I stayed with them for about a year. They helped me a lot. They even paid for the months they'd been away. Over that year I became much stronger. I was very sad when they had to leave again and this time it was for good. They gave me a fantastic reference, and with this experience I thought I'd probably pick up better paid work.

* * *

I was home for about a month when I applied for a job with the Cabrera family in Managua and got it. But that job meant I had to leave Laura with Mum and Ana. The Cabrera family was one of the richest in Nicaragua and working for them was very different from being with the American family.

Señora Cabrera's parties were out of this world. They took days to prepare, and it took months, I kid you not, when it came to her daughter's wedding. Señora Cabrera hired the entire Intercontinental Hotel for the reception, I mean their reception hall, the kitchen, the kitchen staff and their waiters.

On the actual day of the wedding we were sent into the hotel at dawn and from then on we were at it, decorating the hall, placing hundreds of knives and forks, making roses out of the napkins, double-checking to be sure all the place-names were right. Then we rushed off to change. I had a black dress with a frilly white apron and putting on this little hat I hardly recognized myself in the mirror.

It was like a film looking at the guests. A photographer was running about taking pictures of them all arriving and the women were wearing amazing dresses.

We had to take our orders from the head waiter and were going back and forth serving all these rich people capers, soup, lobster, steak, all with champagne, margaritas, rum, beers, and we went on serving through the speeches. It slowed down a bit when the band came on and the dancing started.

When the party was over we had this massive hall to clear up, and the amount of food wasted! Plates and glasses full, even the five-tier wedding cake hadn't been touched other than the knife stuck in for the photo. And it was all thrown away. We had to leave the place spotless so weren't ready to go back to the big house until four in the morning and were back on duty by seven. Normally it was six.

That was how we were treated. Our first meal was at two in the afternoon because we were only allowed to eat after their lunch and often we were eating their leftovers. We existed to serve. I remember feeling so embarrassed when Mum came for the first time to visit me. She rang the front door bell but the butler wouldn't let her in. He told her to use the tradesman's entrance.

At bedtime I'd take the newspaper out of their waste basket to check the ads and when I saw a position in Managua with a Señor Velázquez I openly applied. I knew I was good at my job and they couldn't stop me. I was given an interview and offered the job at three hundred *córdobas*. It was more than I'd ever earned.

The Velázquez family still lives there; I went past their mansion a month back and nothing looks changed. They're big landowners and live a luxurious lifestyle. I hadn't actually been there that long when their doctor, Dr García, asked if they could recommend a maid, so they offered me to go and work for him. I was basically told to accept it but it was less work and the same pay so I was happy. This gave me an extra free day to go home and see Laura.

For a change, one Saturday I went with Paula, the other maid in the house, to her place. It was her girl's birthday and she was putting on a party for her and her little friends. Paula had invited also some of her own pals and she introduced me to this nice-looking man, Rubén. We got chatting and danced some. He said his mum lived in Managua and his dad worked on his holding not far out of town.

After that Paula kept inviting me to her place and it was no coincidence that every time I went, Rubén would appear. Then he began turning up by the side gate to Dr García's house. Rubén sold door-to-door cosmetics, nail varnish and face creams, and would always give me something like a pretty hair band. Then another man called by one day, selling handmade brooms. He introduced himself as Don Valerio and said he was Rubén's dad. He said his son had told him such wonderful things about me that he wanted to meet me. And once he had, he too kept coming by. Every time he came he would talk about his beautiful home, his beautiful holding and about wanting me to visit. I thought, well, why not? So one Saturday I asked Paula to come with me, and who should I find there but Rubén.

That's how we started going out together. Rubén was very kind, always giving me small presents. We sometimes walked about Managua but it was nicer at his father's place. Rubén, though, wanted more than just my free days together. He'd go on about how nice it would be if we had our own place and kept saying, 'Aren't you fed up with that live-in job? Think about it, you could come and live with me at my mum's.' He wanted me at least to visit her and when I did she made me very welcome.

She teased, 'Ah, I'm watching you – you're going to steal my boy.' But Rubén said, 'Oh no, she won't. I like living here. And Dad drinks too much.' That was news to me. Rubén lived with his mum in Managua getting by with his door-to-door cosmetics sales. He also had a part-time security job in town and only sometimes stayed with his dad helping him make his brooms.

I could see his mum had her hands full, she had so many grandchildren, but after that visit Rubén wouldn't rest until I agreed to move in with him. I said I would only if Dr García's wife agreed to me working days, which she did.

Rubén had a room at the back of his mum's place and we made it as nice as we could. I felt like I was on a honeymoon, in a dream world of love, and a few months later I became pregnant.

I suppose that's what woke me up. One of Rubén's sisters had three children, the other had two and there was the younger sister as well. The kids were always yelling, and sharing the patio, the bathroom, and the laundry sink wasn't easy. I began to feel I was living in a dog kennel. It all got to be too much and when his mum started making snide remarks about me coming and going, saying I liked being out too much, I told Rubén we needed to find our own place. He knew I wasn't happy so he agreed. I asked around and a friend of mine offered to rent half of her space, which was perfect other than that we had very little money; what I earned went to keep Laura. But Rubén said not to worry, I could rely on him, so just before I was due, I gave notice and quit my job.

Rubén was over the moon when Darío was born. Yes, we were both very happy. I had Darío in 1975, three years after Laura. I was twenty-two. And we managed; we scraped by on Rubén's wages. But then something began to change for Rubén. I don't know why, but he was drinking.

'What happened to your promise?' I asked.

He wouldn't or couldn't answer. He wouldn't say why and his money kept on disappearing. He was out all the time and when he did come back, he was out of it. Paying the rent for the room was becoming a struggle and in the end something had to give.

I had to go and ask Rubén's mum to mind Darío while I looked for another live-in job. I didn't explain why, I just said money was tight. She said OK and fortunately it didn't take long to find one. It was a neighbour of Tina's, an elderly woman, Doña Paulina, and she was happy for me to move in with Darío. She could do most things for herself and she knew I wanted to visit Rubén on my free days. It was tough on Rubén. He loved me and Darío but he'd left me no choice. Rubén decided then to move out of Managua to his dad's holding and I told him I'd try and visit him with Darío whenever I could.

I had my own room with Darío at the back of Doña Paulina's house, and maybe I'd been there about a month when one night I awoke to this noise: baram, baram, baram. It was far away, a rumbling sound like a cart carrying a load of stones. It got louder and louder and it was really strange how no dogs were barking. The noise got really frightening and loud as it passed the house and slowly, slowly, it faded into the distance.

I couldn't wait to say good morning to Doña Paulina and ask her, 'Did you hear that noise last night?'

'I wanted to come to you,' she said, 'but I was too scared. What a noise and my dogs didn't bark, they were whimpering under the bed.' She had two dogs herself. She said, 'Rosa, you know something very bad is going to happen.'

Doña Paulina was a strong woman so this stayed with me. I didn't know what to think. Nothing seemed untoward to me. If it was the Nahual Cart, I knew it was surely a sign. The Nahual Cart is the spirit of death the Spanish brought at the time of conquest, when they enslaved and killed us.

*The Nahual Cart is the spirit of death*

The next time I saw Rubén I told him all about that night and how Doña Paulina and I were both sure it had been the Cart of Death. He looked really surprised and then said I should leave Managua and move in with him at his dad's place.

'On what?' I asked. I said we'd all be better off if he got a factory job back in Managua, but he said, 'You know how I hate working under a boss.'

When I wasn't seeing Laura in La Concha, I'd go with Darío and spend my weekends with Rubén on his dad's holding. But Rubén's drinking had me wondering why I was bothering. Other than that I'd become good pals with Susana, the daughter of Don Valerio's neighbour. She too came home at weekends and often she'd drop in on Don Valerio for a chat. That's how I got to know her and it turned out we had a lot in common. I invited her to La Concha to meet my family and she'd also visit me at Doña Paulina's in Managua. She took interest in what I thought and was really concerned about how things were between Rubén and me. She could see they weren't great. I listened to her, took her advice. She said, 'Rosa, if you two spent more time together, you might fix your relationship.' She worked in Managua and said she'd tell me if she heard of any day jobs. And it didn't take long before she came to tell me she'd found two homes wanting only washing and ironing done and that would free me to come back every evening to be with Rubén at the holding. I was sorry to have to tell Doña Paulina I was leaving but she knew how things were with Rubén and gave me her blessing. The good thing was I could take Darío with me to these different homes, and I was now living again with Rubén, but I can't say Rubén drank any less.

\* \* \*

I'd been working like this and sleeping over at the farm maybe three months when Susana came to tell me she knew a couple looking for a daytime maid and they'd be fine if I wanted to have Darío with me. From everything she told me about Don Federico and his wife, Inés, I felt I knew them before I went to visit. The wife struck me as really kind. She was a nurse and Federico an engineer. Inés explained to me that they often had friends stay over and would I mind doing the extra washing of sheets if paid the extra. I thought that was very decent; I'd never been offered that before. It showed the sort of people they were so I was happy to accept the job.

And they did treat me well. They gave me my wages on time and I ate the same meals as they did and with them, and by mid-afternoon I was off home to Rubén. It didn't take long because they were on that side of town.

They'd no children of their own and took a real shine to Darío, giving him clothes and toys even though they weren't well-off. In fact they didn't seem to have much at all. Federico said there was little work coming in and I'd often see him napping. And

Inés was certainly right about them having friends to stay. At times it was more like running a guest house.

After some months with them Federico asked if I'd mind the place for the weekend while they went to the beach and offered to pay me and said of course Darío should stay too. He only asked if I'd cook for their friends staying on. So they went off and that evening, after I'd served supper for their guests, I went to bed in a room in the annex.

I woke in the middle of the night to this tick-tick-ticking. I lay there listening, wondering if I should get up and wake one of the guests. I slipped out from my room but stopped in my tracks. Across the patio I could see into the house. One of the guests was typing and the other two were making some posters I think, painting lettering.

I went back to bed and thought maybe it was best not to say anything. I'd have been told by Federico and Inés if I was meant to know something.

And when they did come back life went on like before. I was happy enough going home with Darío every day. I thought Inés very easy-going and welcoming. Quite often Susana dropped by for coffee and we'd chat. One time she asked if I'd go with her to her Parents' Evening after work. She said she thought I might like to see the school with a mind to Darío, and I could catch the later bus back home.

The meeting was the following week at her boy's school. We walked there together and when we arrived in the classroom, there were only a few parents. Susana then introduced me. 'This is Rosa, she works for Federico.'

I couldn't make sense of anything that was being talked about, but this was definitely no 'Parents' Evening'. And what Federico had to do with this I had no idea. He had nothing to do with the school or the children, so as soon as we got out I asked Susana.

She wouldn't say, she just started on about there being no freedom in Nicaragua and life being worthless.

'What's that to do with anything? Why did you take me there?'

'So you'd join us.'

'Join what?'

'Join us. Join in with the people at the meeting.'

'What are you on about?'

'Rosa, what don't you see? There are people everywhere, all over the country, working to get rid of the dictator.'

Crazy! That's what I thought: she's totally crazy.

I left Susana feeling very put out and took the bus home with Darío. I then had time to think. 'Best quit my job.' But I didn't say a word about this to Rubén.

As soon as I got to the house the next day I asked Federico if I might have a word. I told him, 'I can't go on working here. My husband wants me to leave. I've got to go.'

'But what happened? Susana sent you here on such good recommendations. You're such a fine person, and we know we can depend on you. I know you can be trusted.' Oh, if you heard Federico talk, he'd persuade you of anything, but no, I wasn't having it, not until he said, 'Listen Rosa, the truth is you can't leave now. You know too much.'

I felt cold. 'So you've trapped me. You never told me what I was letting myself into.' At least he had the decency to admit it. He went on. 'I know you're angry now but I also know you want a better life for Darío and Laura. That's what this struggle is for. We're doing this for our children's future. You're a woman of principles and I tell you, we really need you.'

I was raging. 'You say that but you've given no thought about my Darío, me and Rubén.'

Don Federico was sure of himself. 'You won't lose Rubén or Darío. But between you and me, I want you to make sure not to say anything to Rubén or anyone else about this.'

I was trying to grasp all this when he said, 'Now you're on the inside, you'd be safer staying here during the week.' I was in no position to argue. I only said, 'Then the one thing I ask is that you never do anything to endanger Darío's life.'

That evening I went home but all I said to Rubén was that I'd be paid more if I lived at Federico's during the week and they were happy for Darío to be with me. It was strange; it was as if we'd come to some kind of unsaid understanding. Rubén simply said, 'Do what you feel you have to. If you have to live in, you have to.'

I wasn't happy. Susana, Federico, Inés, they'd all deceived me. You need to know that the Sandinistas didn't always recruit by explaining things first. They recruited many by indirect means. That's how the Sandinista organization grew, meeting secretly in small groups in churches, schools and other places. I realized Susana had been checking me out, all those questions, asking about my work, and how I tried to study and what I knew about town. Really she was seeing if I had what it took and obviously decided I did, so then she dropped me in it. Once I knew too much I had no way out.

It was complicated. Susana had a big influence on me, she made me more aware. I think her political thinking started with being part of the Popular Church. She'd been in the Sandinista underground movement a long time. What she said was right about what I'd gone through in those big houses. I'd told her about when Mum first came to see me at Doña Cabrera's and the butler telling me, 'Rosa, it's prohibited for any visitor of yours to be seen at the front door. They can come only at ten in the morning and stay for five minutes only.' Here was my mother, after a long journey, and she couldn't stay more than five minutes. I only had time to give her what money I had and tell her when I'd next have a day off and ask, 'How's my girl?' And when I went to work for Dr García, it was the same. We weren't allowed a bite until his last guest left and we'd cleared up. And being told by their butler, 'That plate isn't for you. What you use is underneath,' pointing to metal dishes kept for the dogs! I remembered all these things. Talking to Susana I realized how demeaning all this was.

And I talked often with young René, who sometimes stayed at the house. He'd ask, wouldn't I like to become a nurse or a secretary? Of course, I said, but the question was how. And I would think about the life for most people; most folk didn't have any schooling, never mind the luxury of water and electricity, and only ever knew beans and rice to eat, like cows eating to survive. All I knew was being a maid and cleaner. I had never thought there was anything but the rich being rich and the poor being poor, and that was life, just like Somoza and his family ruled the country and always would.

Susana and Federico made sense. I'd never discussed working conditions or that there should be a minimum wage with anyone before. I'd never thought about human rights, much less having a union to protect those rights. I'd known nothing about the Sandinistas or what they were fighting for, never mind a safe house – nothing.

Overnight my life had been turned upside down. Now I was working with Susana in her clandestine cell in her *barrio* and everything had to be kept secret. I learned all about security matters, the Sandinistas' tactics and how they were organized. When I became involved, the Sandinistas were already a big network.

This was in 1977 and I had to be very careful. Now I knew what Federico and Inés were really doing, but to anyone else I was just the maid getting on with the washing. Everyone kept their personal secret. We all changed our names and where we grew up: I was Diana from León. Now I was taking messages and small arms to different locations. I would still try to see Rubén but he knew nothing. It had to be that way.

We had to do a lot of things for security reasons; we had to move so often I got to know nearly every *barrio* in Managua. It was becoming riskier by the day. People were disappearing or being imprisoned, and for nothing. Shootings and killings were happening everywhere. Somoza's National Guard suspected everyone of being a collaborator, even small children, and as the situation worsened children did start joining. The boy next door disappeared. He was thirteen and we found out he had taken part in an assault.

We had to depend a lot on the Recuperation Brigades for our food. They looted shops and raided a supermarket, stealing sugar, beans and oil to give to the Sandinista cells. And all these people involved in the struggle were good people. Without them I'm not sure how we'd have eaten.

It was becoming so dangerous in Managua that Don Federico told me it would be safer for Darío to be in La Concha. I should have listened to him and taken Darío there and then but I didn't want to be separated from him. Darío was only two. Instead the following weekend I went with Darío to see his dad and that's when Darío fell out of the hammock and came down with a fever. He was so ill I took him to hospital and stayed with him for two days. He was put on a drip but he wasn't much better when I left with him. I had to get back to Don Federico; there were things I had to do.

Two weeks later Darío wasn't much better and Federico again advised he'd be safer with my mum. This time I agreed and the following weekend I took Darío to La Concha. Mum could see how he was and said she'd take care of him. When I went back to La Concha the following week, Darío seemed well enough, playing, eating and sleeping OK, so I wasn't too worried. And now I was free to do more, Federico gave me a lot more responsibility.

It was for the best. I'd talked to Susana about this, about the risks we ran being messengers for the Sandinistas. We had an agreement that if she was killed I would take on her children and she would do the same for me. We were living with fear and it was becoming harder to visit home.

In 1978 the fighting intensified. Throughout that year it became an ever tighter circle of fear. I'd try to visit La Concha whenever I could, taking the bus at the end of the day with the market women, to be part of the crowd, and leave first thing in the morning. My family knew nothing but Mum worried. 'Rosa, why are you leaving this early?'

'I have to be back to serve breakfast.'

'You must stop running about like this, it's too dangerous out there,' she said and she was right. Mum worried a lot about what she called the 'bandits'. 'Ah, these bandits are everywhere, on the Masaya road, the San Marcos road.'

I tried to send home provisions because otherwise they'd have had no rice or oil. Dad could put some beans and maize on the table with what he grew, but going to Managua to sell had become impossible, so they had no money.

That year Pedro Joaquín Chamorro was murdered. Chamorro was a leader of a party opposing the dictator and his murder caused a massive protest. People braved it, coming out in a general strike; everyone wanted Somoza gone. Then in August a Sandinista Commando unit seized the National Palace and demanded the release of Sandinista prisoners. When they won this, it was clear to everyone that the dictator wasn't in total control.

For months I didn't see Rubén. I was still delivering messages and arms here and there and it wasn't until Easter the following year, in 1979, that I saw him. We spent a whole two days together. It was only then he told me that for years he'd known about folk going missing, disappearing, and that's why he'd moved out of Managua. He'd known there were death squads, seen them with his own eyes. He said he'd seen bodies dumped on waste ground. But why hadn't he told me? That was why he'd gone to stay on his father's plot. He begged again, 'You don't rest, you don't eat. Please stay here on the holding.'

'No, I can't.'

It was that Easter I became pregnant with Angélica.

The Sandinistas were fighting now in Granada, Masaya, León, Estelí and Matagalpa. That year in April was the 'Final Offensive' and Somoza's National Guard was being stretched thin. Small towns like La Concha were now left open and one night the Sandinistas came in the early hours. The *muchachos* threw a chain over the electricity lines, causing a blackout, and then they attacked the Guard's military post. We woke to the noise of explosions, grenades and shooting.

Next morning the *Guardia* did a house-to-house search, but by then the *muchachos* were long gone.

And so was I. That was how it was; we had to kick up a dust storm. I was running here and there, staying sometimes over at Susana's, sometimes Federico's. And my baby; I worried that I might miscarry.

*And my baby; I worried that I might miscarry*

I didn't go home again until the beginning of June. Federico had received enough provisions to give me a sack of bread, cheese, sugar and some soap.

'See if you can take that home,' he said.

Someone from our cell said he'd give me a lift as he was going nearby, to San Marcos. Mum was so glad for the food and Rubén was there; he'd come from his dad's place to see Darío. I got stuck in La Concha. Fighting had broken out on the main road into Managua so I had no way to get back. I felt dreadful and Rubén could see this. He begged me, 'Why risk it, please, come back with me.' I told him that if I had to get out of Managua, I'd find him.

That's how we left things and I managed to return to Federico's two days later.

It was then the house on the South Highway in Managua was raided. It was more than luck none of us were there. The *Guardia* took maps and papers but found no weapons.

We moved instantly to another safe house and from there to another, and it was there Federico decided we had to disband. He said we were marked and had to disperse, and that he'd send word if we were to regroup.

Susana was my contact and she took me to her parents. I still didn't know about the arms cache she had there. Only later did I find out that was why she kept visiting home, to store guns on the land, and her father knew nothing.

Susana told her mum I'd been given a break from work, making out I wanted a rest too from my kids. I was there only a couple of days when a neighbour came to warn them that the *Guardia* were in the area. I'd have compromised the family so I gave some excuse, saying I was off to visit Don Valerio and took off. Goodness knows what they really thought. Rubén was there and was very happy to see me. I'm sure his dad knew more than he let on. He was very careful.

Susana came a week later to tell me to go to friends of Federico, 'Maritza' and 'Ramón' in Managua, and we left separately. Maritza wasn't her real name. I could tell by her accent she came from the north, the Matagalpa region. She was fair and pretty. She said, 'If anyone asks, you're my cleaner and Ramón, he's my husband.'

I stayed there during the fiercest of the fighting. The *Guardia* were bombing Estelí, León and Jinotepe. It was life or death. Folk were building road blocks to stop the tanks but no one was safe. In Estelí the *Guardia* cut off the water and electricity. People risked everything for a bucket of water. It was us or them. The fighting was everywhere. And thousands of people fled Managua that June. They all left one night to escape the onslaught, disappearing from the *barrios* and walking all the way to Masaya.

In mid-July I left too. I managed to get a lift to near Rubén's place, to the Monte Tabor Church. I could hear firing nearby and escaped inside the church. Soon as I stepped inside I felt overwhelmed by grief. The sound of all the women and children praying filled the church and I sat down with them. Everyone was praying for an end to the war, for an end to the fighting. There was Christ shining on the Cross, lit by a hundred candles. I don't know how long I sat there praying. 'Dearest María, Somoza isn't letting go, he won't give in. He's bombing women and children, killing our sons. Please, no more, let this war end. How many more wounded, how many more killings will there have to be? Our families are breaking; there's no food, no money.' I said, 'This must end.'

It was starting to get dark when I came out of the church and the place had gone quiet. I bought some oranges from a woman selling by the church door and hurried on to Don Valerio's place.

Rubén was shocked to see me. 'Rosa, how did you get here? You could have been shot. Didn't you hear the firing?' And this time when he begged, 'Now please don't think of going back,' I said, 'I won't. Managua's too dangerous.'

We went to bed and stayed up talking about Laura and Darío. I said depending on how things went that week, I'd try and go see them at the weekend. Rubén said I could take some of the squash his dad was growing.

I told him about the church, the women praying and how I felt something would happen soon and then must have fallen asleep.

A-BOOM, boom, boom. I woke to hear the explosions. 'Dear God, the people in Managua; they're being bombed.' I got up and ran out. It was dawn and some lads were running along the path, shouting, 'Somoza is gone, Somoza's fled.'

'No, these lads are drunk,' Rubén said and took down his dad's transistor off the shelf above the stove. Radio Corporación was the only station you could get. And we listened. 'Latest news! Latest news! Somoza has fled the country.' This was Somoza's official radio station. All other stations were clandestine and you'd only get those at, say, one in the morning. Day and night Somoza's was the only voice you heard, so when we heard Somoza was gone we knew the Sandinistas had taken the station. The broadcast went on, 'Go to the plaza. This is the day of our victory; this is the day of our happiness.'

'Is this really possible?' I wondered. 'Yesterday I prayed for Somoza to go and today he's gone!' Had God heard the people's prayers?

We kept listening to the radio, hearing people were gathering in the main square in Managua. The next day, July 18, we heard that groups of Sandinistas were rounding up Somoza's Guardsmen who hadn't fled the country. I kept my ear to the radio and when I heard that all Sandinista troops would be converging in the plaza the next day, I told Rubén I was going. But even then I didn't tell him how much a part of this I was. He said, 'No, don't go. You'll be killed.'

'No, why am I going to be killed? Not now!' But he wasn't far wrong. Next morning I walked to the main road and hitched a lift on a lorry. They said they were going to the plaza. 'Come on, get on.' They were picking up people from here and there and down a back road they got held up by a funeral procession. Some of these people started yelling. 'You Sandinista bastards, you killed our son!'

It was turning nasty. The lorry had been forced to stop so I jumped off and ran for it, back to the main road.

When I finally got to Managua I walked to the plaza. It was a sea of people, all smiling and also many in tears, tears of happiness and tears of grief.

I looked and looked but saw no one I knew.

I needed to know who was still alive.

Yes, tears of happiness, tears of grief.

I went to find Federico and he told me René had been killed, he'd been shot two days before the victory. René had been with us throughout all the fighting. He'd been a messenger like me, travelling from one place to another to deliver messages and weapons.

He died too young.

## María

The man who took our land, Domingo, was my Aunt Brígida's son. She had married Lorenzo. Year after year Lorenzo had bought land, so by the time he died Brígida was left a farm.

She never stopped working. Every week she killed a pig to make pork *nacatamales*. That business made her plenty more money, enough to send Domingo to the University of León. When Domingo returned home, he was an educated man.

He took up a good position in the Law Court in Masaya and soon he married a lady called Idania and they had three children. When they grew up he could afford for them to have a university education too.

And all during those years he too acquired more and more land until he had three large farms. In time he resigned from the Law Court to dedicate himself to his coffee, coconuts, mandarins and oranges and he hired many farmhands. They worked for him, caring for his fruit trees and clearing his land of undergrowth,

41

and in return he'd give them time to eat, but that was all. He wouldn't even give them a stick of firewood.

It must be ten years since Brígida had her stroke. She was left paralyzed and needed twenty-four-hour care. Domingo paid a woman to look after her until she passed away. And it was then, after his mother's death, that his life narrowed.

We watched as his lands grew wild. He was no longer seen on his farm, El Jardín. He left it all to the birds and monkeys.

He lived within the walls of the farmhouse until Idania also died. Then he too took ill, ending his days in a wheelchair. He died five years after his mother. Domingo was mean of spirit and mean of life, and why?

* * *

I've seen it's the educated men who get on. Don Victor next door, he was once mayor of La Concha and kept company with Ramón Solís and José María Salas. Don Salas was one of the biggest landowners, like Domingo. They, along with Don Montoya, ran the town affairs. Don Montoya is Serafina's father, and she's now the Sandinista leader here. They have a house in Granada. My daughter Flor said her husband Enrique was doing a carpentry job for them, putting up shelving and saw sacks and sacks of rice and sugar there in their house, and you do ask yourself why.

After the revolution in 1979 Serafina was elected mayor. The revolution saw most of these men I mentioned lose their positions. José María Salas, he left before the Sandinistas took over and I see Uriel Vásquez just wandering around his farm. But René Colón, he was sent to prison for thirty years. He was a man who had condemned the innocent instead of the guilty. Somoza installed him here as the town mayor. There were no clean elections then;

that's how Somoza ruled. There was no justice, but nor was there before the Somoza family came to rule the country.

When I was a girl La Concha was under the command of one man, a man we called El Buey, the Ox. We called him that because he was a beast of a man. He was head of the district's *Guardia* and he and his men controlled the whole district. Everyone was frightened of him. Mother bolted the doors whenever we heard his men were in town. They'd break into our homes and steal the cane liquor, the *chicha* we made.

He looted and robbed from San Marcos to Masatepe and La Concha. No one could stand in his way. Justo Buey sold the *chicha*, it was his contraband business and no one could stop him. He'd come and take whatever and whoever he wanted.

One night my brother Ernesto hadn't come home and we heard Buey was in town. Mother stayed up waiting and when I heard her shout I got up and ran through. Ernesto was covered in blood. Together we cleaned and bandaged the cuts he had to his arms. He said he'd heard screaming when heading home through Barrio Santiago, and went with the men coming with machetes, hurrying to where the screaming was coming from. He said they shouted for Buey to come out but he didn't, so they broke in. Buey and his men were wild and drunk and they'd taken the women of the house.

The fighting was fierce, he said. They fought hard and when they killed Justo Buey, his men fled. They dragged Buey out of the house and pulled him onto his horse, and that's when they saw Justo Buey had tattooed the image of the Devil on his chest and on his back. The men tied him down and sent the horse packing.

For a long time Buey's spirit remained wandering around La Concha and it was a spirit in torment. Father had seen this; he'd come home late one evening and heard what sounded like a child crying. He thought a child was lost and went to look but what he

43

*The image of the Devil on his chest and on his back*

saw in the dusk was a beast kicking and wailing, then in a flash it turned and fled. I went to talk to our priest about this and he said in time his spirit would go.

My husband preferred not to speak of such occurrences at all, especially in front of the children, and I agreed. He had his experience of such an occurrence that had left him very shaken. This was after he'd been to a wake and was walking back in early morning. He heard rustling and turned. A woman was walking some way behind him with a lit candle on her head. He said she'd cast a spell for the faster he walked, the less ground he covered and the closer she came. It was then, as she drew near, that she suddenly vanished into thin air. And in that instant, he regained his step and was able to walk but when he arrived home he was trembling. She was a witch.

*The faster he walked, the less ground he covered*

One of these two witches we had here in La Concha could turn herself into a monkey. She did this to steal. She stole chickens, turkeys, even pigs, and she was such a nuisance that some folk went to our priest to ask what to do. He told them to use the cord from the statue of San Francisco and to lay it across the path she was known to take, and scatter mustard seeds there and shoe tacks. This way, he said, she'd be caught. And sure enough, the next morning she was found there tangled up in the Saint's cord, scratching and rolling about in the path. These people then took her to the priest in the church and I was told that when he untied the cord of the Saint, she died there and then. She must have died from shame. This happened when I was very young.

\* \* \*

Nowadays stealing is done by quite another type of person and that's why I've told you these things, to explain why you must live with a clear conscience. Then nothing bad will happen to you. If you pray, pray from your heart, Christ hears you. When you pray from your heart and pray with a clear conscience for a good life, you'll be given a good life; and if you pray to Christ to heal the sick, he will help them recover.

You know, don't you, how important it is to live with a good conscience? You will then have a pure spirit. I pray every day and look to live in peace. And this has been my life and look how blessed I am with all my children still alive.

There have been few difficulties. Yes, maybe a few problems with my neighbour, Esmeralda, Victor's wife. I'd say we've reached an understanding. A trouble that I'm sorry to say started way back when Rosa was at school and Esmeralda's girl had a fight with her in the playground.

I told the girl, 'Rosa is much smaller than you. You're naughty to hit her and if I hear you've done this again, I'll have words with your father.'

She didn't even say sorry. Instead she told her mother I'd spanked her and from then on Esmeralda seemed to be the one offended. She had her worries, mind you. I saw Don Victor drunk often enough and I knew his doctor was visiting the house regularly until he passed away.

It was then that Esmeralda took it into her head that Don Victor had been cursed and sent her daughter to San Cristóbal, near the coast, to see a medium. Esmeralda is from there and too many from there are not true followers of the Catholic faith. Esmeralda … there's no other way to put this: she's rather odd. She's said some nasty things and took it into her head that I held a grudge against her husband. Why she's so bitter I don't know.

But when her girl came back she told her mother she'd seen a medium and the woman had confirmed what the girl asked, that Don Victor had been cursed, and what's more added that their home was full of spirits.

Esmeralda then began seeing ghosts. She came to tell me she'd seen a dwarf sitting on her door lintel. Then she said she'd found a glass jar containing a little figure with pins stuck into it buried in her garden. But I never saw this; she never showed me.

She said I was the one responsible. She implied I had cursed him, had put the glass jar in their garden, dear me. I don't know how she could accuse me of such a thing! Don Victor was related to my family. Everyone told me to ignore her and not to worry. 'We know Esmeralda. She doesn't know what she's on about.'

This nonsense was only ended by Esmeralda's Aunt Marta. Bless her, she was on her death bed when she called for both of us to come and see her. It was the day she passed away. She said her dying wish was to see this trouble end. She said to Esmeralda, 'You know Doña María didn't do any of these things you talk about. You know they're all lies. Before I depart from this world I need to hear you apologize to her.' And Esmeralda, she did apologize.

That cleared the air and we remained on good terms, going together to do our washing in Lake Venecia.

# 2 Fireworks

*A year has passed. It is 1988 and the Contra rebels, much weakened, are forced to negotiate a peace. But it has taken a punishing toll on the country. People are exhausted and there are the first signs of disillusionment.*

## Rosa

Everyone was talking to each other about things they'd never dared mention before – the loved ones they'd lost, their sorrow and grief, the ways they'd messed up. I think everyone was releasing tensions or stress. It was like an endless explosion of fireworks; everything bottled up, everything we'd gone through came pouring out. And this gave us freedom. It was real and beautiful. It was unforgettable. Joining the crowd in the plaza on July 19, 1979, was a day I'll always treasure.

The dictatorship had ruled Nicaragua for forty-three years and at last it was over. Somoza had fled to Miami.

Everyone talked about what they'd gone through. It was as if waking up from a long nightmare. And I was very happy. Yes, happiness mixed with relief and grief. Oh, the pain when I heard what had happened to René. He had been killed two days before the triumph – only two days – caught in an ambush on the Masaya Highway, near the Santiago Volcano. We had got to know each other. I was like a sister to him. I'd done his washing for him. He was a gentle soul. I wanted to find his family to visit them and give them my condolences, but no one knew where they lived.

Dad was right, the young had given everything. He'd said, 'We should have fought Somoza when we were young, not left this battle for our children to fight.' Fifty thousand people had died. There are still many unmarked graves in the country. Our parents were blessed not to lose any of us. Marcos and Sergio too had gone missing in those last months. Dad had told them not to leave La Concha, then we heard there'd been a shootout in Jinotepe. A local Sandinista was reported killed. It happened as they were retreating to El Crucero.

It turns out Marcos and Sergio had been with him but they'd somehow escaped and hid in the hills out there, then made their way home at night. They reached home after three days but said nothing about this at the time, instead making up some story. I only found out after the victory, when Marcos told us all. I had no idea they were in the Sandinista cell in La Concha and they hadn't a clue about me.

I was in Managua staying with Susana and went to see if Rubén was at his mum's place. This was when I told him about my involvement. He listened but he was angry.

'Why didn't you ever tell me? You could have been killed! Don't you care anything for your children, or me?'

'You can't think that! Do you think I did this for some crazy adventure? I did it for the children's future.'

'We didn't have to fight; life is fine on Dad's farm,' he said. And then his mum piped up. 'Rosa, you're young. The Sandinistas, they took advantage of you.'

'Yes, you could be right there,' I said, 'so I'd fight for your rights.'

'Dear me, what are you on about, chasing some fantasy of freedom.'

She said it, didn't she? 'Yes, you're correct, I want freedom and I've won it.'

Rubén wasn't happy but that's how it was. And I was. I had this great feeling, walking the streets fearing nothing; it was a *fiesta*, to talk with ease to everyone and anyone, women and men.

Yes, it was an awakening. And for me personally, I was never ever going to work as a maid again, no, not for anyone. The revolution opened doors for me I never thought possible and would take me places I'd never gone before.

I was offered a proper job in a proper workplace with proper wages. It was a real opportunity, though I knew nothing would come easy. The job was in a new print shop and I started out learning how to process film for the printing plates.

I was very pregnant now with Angélica and feeling on that wave of the revolution that everything would work out. Dad offered Rubén a chance to join his cooperative in La Concha and farm alongside him. It meant me travelling to work but for Rubén it seemed a good plan so we moved into the house back home and Rubén joined the farm workers' union, the ATC. I was commuting to Managua every day and kept working until I was very nearly due. I was frightened at the thought of delivering at home and told Rubén I wanted to give birth in a hospital in Managua. I'd already asked my brother-in-law, Alfonso, if he'd take me to Managua. He said he'd be happy to. He'd been given a confiscated police jeep and loved driving around in it.

But nothing goes to plan. My contractions started in the early hours and I told Rubén I would go and catch the first bus out to Managua. He said I was mad: 'You'll end up giving birth on the bus.'

No matter, I was off and caught the early morning bus. I was no further than the edge of town when I heard this beep, beep, beeping and a jeep zoomed by and forced the bus driver to stop.

Alfonso then leapt on board with Rubén, Alfonso in his Sandinista Police uniform, and Rubén saying, 'Come on, Rosa, get off.' I was mortified, saying to everyone, 'I'm so sorry, I'm going to have a baby,' and all the passengers staring. I'm sure they thought I was being arrested.

By five in the morning I was in a bed at the Vélez Paiz Hospital. The attention was fantastic; I was seen to immediately. There were a lot of doctors, many from abroad, and they took great care of me. Maybe because of the tension I'd held back, the contractions kept going on and on, until two in the afternoon. The doctor joked, 'Your baby's a lazy girl. She needs waking up.' They had to induce her but thankfully a caesarean wasn't needed.

She nearly asphyxiated because she had passed her time. She should have been born at ten at the latest. She was born purple but they gave her a good smack on her bum, and hah, then she cried and the doctor had to put an apparatus in her mouth and drain liquid.

Angélica had to struggle to come into the world. This was five months after the triumph, in December of 1979. Hers was not an easy birth. Yes, Angélica is a child of the revolution and it was only because of their attention that she didn't die. This was thanks to what we'd fought for and was something truly marvellous.

When we came back to La Concha I stayed home looking after Angélica and Rubén worked with Dad clearing land on the farm. So much land had gone wild because of the war. Rubén seemed to feel part of the ATC, going to their meetings.

Three months later, I too was back working and Mum took care of Angélica at home. I was off at five in the morning and wasn't back until seven at night. For a year we managed like this but we were too crowded in the one space so Mum suggested that Rubén and I build our own home next to the house. We could only afford planks of wood. It was very basic, a wooden shed with no foundation or anything solid, but it was our family home.

We'd been living like this for maybe six months when one evening I came back and in the dusk I could just make out a load of cement blocks piled up where our room had been.

I went into the house and found Ana. I asked her what had happened.

'Marcos brought those building materials,' she said.

'But why?'

'He's going to build his house there,' she said.

'And Dad didn't say anything?'

'Yes, he did. He told Marcos to put the blocks where they are after pulling down your room.'

I found Mum in the kitchen but she'd only say, 'It was your father's decision.'

I knew she wasn't going to differ but she wouldn't explain why. No explanation and there were my things piled up and nowhere to put my bed. I felt wretched. Thank goodness Rubén was over at his dad's place and didn't come home that night.

But when he did, next day, I told him what had happened and Rubén just said, 'I want nothing more to do with here. My dad has land enough for us to build our home there. You decide what you want to do, come or stay, but I'm leaving now.'

I don't know if there'd been a falling out between Dad and him or what, but Rubén was just as upset as me. I felt this left me no choice but to move to his dad's place near Monte Tabor. Moving everything there, especially with Angélica and Darío, was hard going. The holding was along a path a kilometre and a half from the main road.

Don Valerio was very welcoming. 'You'll be fine here. There's plenty of space to build yourselves a room.' And little by little we did, and this time we could afford cement blocks.

It was the walk at dawn and coming home in the dark I didn't like and that never got easier. I had to ask a niece of Rubén's to mind the children but often she couldn't and then I had to rely on Darío to care for Angélica, which wasn't fair on him. He was only six years old and I was having to leave him minding Angélica. But stopping work wasn't an option, and I didn't want to either.

Rubén was working with his dad on the holding but he started wasting any money he earned on playing cards, gambling and drinking. And nor was he being a dad for his children. It was a very emotional time. He'd end up selling the beans below cost or giving away the corn in exchange for a bottle of rum. At least his own dad saw we ate and had the cow's milk cheap. But this getting by wasn't what I wanted. I didn't want my children limited by this life. For a start there was no school there. Rubén agreed that we should move. At the time the Sandinista government was giving out land for housing in what became Barrio Naraja and I decided to sign up. Barrio Naraja became a pilot project for many other *barrios*. Most of the neighbourhood was built on empty ground that Somoza had owned. The *barrio* was built initially in an emergency to house hundreds of families left homeless after a week of torrential rains we had in 1982. All the poorest *barrios* around the shore of Lake Managua had been flooded, leaving these desperate folk with nothing. They were evacuated here with the help of lots of volunteers, the poorest of the poor, and came with nothing.

The Housing Ministry only accepted my application thanks to a reference letter I got from the CST, the Sandinista Trade Union Central. It explained that I needed to live in Managua because of the demands of my job.

This didn't mean we had a house to move into; no, like everyone else we had to build it and this is it. We brought our bed to the plot, Rubén and I, and worked through rain and shine until we had the four posts dug in, then we nailed on the wooden panels. We ate and slept under a plastic cover until we'd secured the roof with corrugated sheeting.

\* \* \*

Then Angélica and Darío moved in and we were at last in our very own home. Laura was twelve years old now and liked school in La Concha and living with my mum, so she stayed there. We moved into the *barrio* just as Darío was due to start school. I enrolled him in the new school in the *barrio* and that was when I found out about his problem. He couldn't cope in class. He showed signs of being different from the other children; he wasn't playing with them and couldn't seem to focus on his learning.

I took him to a doctor who prescribed tranquillizers but that only made him sleepy, and when the drug wore off he became hyper active and aggressive. I then thought to try a herbal cure and took him on the bus to Masaya to see a woman there famous for her remedies. She thought he only had parasites and told me to give him plenty of vitamins, eggs, fruit and salad, but on what money? It was our union social worker who suggested La Mascota, the new free children's hospital. If only I'd thought; it was the obvious and best place, but as it was brand new I didn't know about it.

Darío was seen there by a neurologist and a psychologist. They examined him and afterwards they told me he had a cerebral lesion. This was his problem. We talked about how it might have come about and I realized his condition went back to that time he'd fallen out of the cot. We didn't know at the time but Darío's fever was meningitis.

I blame myself. His illness was in some ways a result of my 'work'; my not getting to hospital fast enough and the chaos in the hospital then were probably why he wasn't correctly diagnosed.

They recommended he go to the special school in Managua and made a referral. It's been excellent for him. It's the only school of its kind. He comes across as timid but he does know himself, has his own intelligence. He's kind, polite and likes his routine.

He's come a long way since he first went there in '83. He has learned to read and the school has helped him feel relaxed with the other children, to get along. He plays with his classmates and can hold a conversation.

He picks up what I show him too. He dresses himself now. The school teaches the children carpentry, dressmaking, hairdressing and basic electric circuits, skills that aren't too taxing. When he leaves at fifteen he'll hopefully be able to find work.

The school was originally set up back in Somoza's days by families who had disabled children. You can see their plaques above the classroom doors. Now it's open to any child with a disability. Many there are children who've been brought out of the war zones, children traumatized by this fighting against the Contra.

I can afford the fees, they're next to nothing. Parents are only asked to give what they can, like textbooks, pens, that kind of thing. It's such a weight off my mind knowing he's there and not roaming about the *barrio*.

And my job is great. I've been learning new things: film and plate processing and now printing, a job with real opportunities. I had asked to be moved to the late shift to have more time with the children but when I did, it was too tiring. After a year I went back to day shift and had to ask Mum to take Angélica for a while. Darío stayed with me though, because of his problems and being at his good school.

The *barrio* has improved a lot. When we moved in it seemed anything that needed doing could be done. When we came, we didn't have a Catholic church so we asked a Jesuit priest to come and he did. From then on he gave Mass in people's homes. That's how the church began in the *barrio*. Everyone was involved in keeping the *barrio* clean and helping with the health prevention work, whatever was going on.

But not Rubén. I'd say to him, 'Will you lend a hand with the vaccination campaign?' but he'd just say, 'Why bust a gut, what for?' He wasn't even interested enough to take Angélica for her vaccinations, and all our neighbours were having their children inoculated. This was the first ever national immunization programme against polio, smallpox and measles.

I'd made friends with Rigoberta and we went around the America One, America Two and Via Venezuela *barrios* to find what could serve as temporary clinics. We went together regularly to the meetings on Sundays, to help make posters showing where to go.

I should tell too about the other major problem in Nicaragua: lack of education. The Literacy Campaign in 1980 was huge; it appealed to all the students to give their time to teach people to read and write, to volunteer to go wherever they were needed and it was incredible how many did.

My youngest brother, Carlos, wanted to go. He was very keen to be one of these teachers and he wasn't going to be stopped. Mum said he couldn't wash or cook but of course he could. When he came back he said this was the most beautiful experience. It was his first time so far from home. He said the families wanted to learn. Carlos was all fired up to become a proper teacher, which is what he became.

* * *

I don't know why but Rubén had no time for anything like that. He wouldn't come to any community activities other than boozing together with some other guys.

I asked Rubén, 'Didn't your dad ever tell you to make a go of life? Have you no ambition? At least get a job. You can't hang around like some ornament.'

I asked at the printers if there was anything going and found him a security job, which he held down for nearly three years till his drinking got the better of him. He'd look to pass the time drinking with one of his mates there until he was caught one night asleep on the job.

It wasn't working. I could see I'd be better off single. At work I heard about AMNLAE, the Luisa Amanda Espinoza Nicaraguan Women's Association, and that woke me up to what a burden he was. I suppose I'd moved on. Perhaps I'm how I am because of the way the Cabreras treated me when I was a maid. I'd fought for these changes and was really happy in my new job. Rubén wasn't, though, and he was never there when I needed him.

I'll tell you what it was like. After I had Angélica I thought best to not risk another pregnancy and decided to have that operation to stop any more. I was left with terrible pains and I had to rest so I went to Mum's. Rubén came too but not because of me; he was going to the wake of a relative of his in La Concha and went off early in the evening to play cards and drink.

That night poor Angélica cried all night long. She wasn't well either but in my condition I could barely lift her and poor Mum was left having to comfort her.

At dawn Rubén walked in, asking for a cup of coffee. But when I said I needed help with Angélica he said, 'I'm not staying around to hear that' and walked off again.

Next time he needs me, I thought, I'll show him, and of course that didn't take long to happen. We were back home in Managua and he had a raging hangover and asked me to go buy him a beer, a hair of the dog. I went off to market and bought what we needed and when I came back I found him shaking and sweating. But I'd 'forgotten' the beer. 'Now you'll remember what it feels like when you need a little help.' Oh, was he mad at me. There are lots of things like that he'll remember me for but nothing worked to stop his drinking.

Dad had told me I was wasting my time trying to change him. The last time I saw Dad he said to me, 'Rosa, listen, you must leave Rubén. You'll never ever be happy staying with him.' And even after Dad had died, he again told me to leave Rubén. He came to me in my sleep. I could see the two of them clear as clear: Dad sitting in the rocking chair and my husband asleep beside me.

'What's this, Rosa?' Dad said. 'Why is Rubén still with you? Why hasn't he gone yet?'

When I woke up I had such a sense of comfort knowing Dad was still around, and that he was making me face up to my relationship. It took one more of Rubén's binges to make me finally tell him.

'The way I see things, if I survived the fighting alone and was able to carry Angélica alone through it all, why now, with a well-paid secure job, can't I raise the children by myself? I'll manage fine without you.'

He had no answer. That was how sad it was and that's how we went our separate ways. He moved back to his father's holding.

I've asked myself many times why he had become so distant. He was a man who had faults but I could live with him. He didn't tell me what to do. He had been kind and gentle. I think it probably built up, like relationships do, from him feeling I didn't trust him because I had kept so much from him during the fight against Somoza. He'd set himself apart.

I can't say I miss him, then or since, and it's been five years. I know he minds not being with the children. He comes occasionally to visit but he's always had one too many and that upsets Darío and Angélica. He's not well. His problem started with his dad. Rubén started drinking when just a lad, he was only twelve.

When his dad came to try to persuade me to take him back, I told him, 'I'm not wasting my life. I've three kids to bring up, they're my priority. You know why Rubén's this way; he started drinking when he was too young to know better. You set him on his path and he's going to go on suffering, but not me. I tried to make it work for too long, but no more.'

I also felt I had lived up to Dad's expectations. I feel he protects me. The night he passed away he came to me in my dream to tell me why he had died. He said he had lost the will to live and had given up. He'd been to see Carlos, to take him a food parcel. Carlos was in the mountains in the north; he'd been conscripted to do his military service and was in Wiwilí fighting the Contra. Dad got a lift with the army and travelled there in an army truck. It took him two days to reach their base but he had only one day with his son before Carlos was sent on another mission.

Dad saw their conditions, how they existed, and Carlos told him how they had to walk for days on end in the rain and sleep wherever, always wet; and the fighting, the skirmishes with the Contra.

When Dad got back home, he stopped eating and took to his bed. He'd never done that in his life. He died in December 1984. Had he not gone he'd be with us today.

When this happened I sent a message to Carlos over the military radio. I hoped he'd pick it up and request compassionate leave. I don't know why he never got the message. He only received the news two weeks later when a friend of Dad's was going that way and went especially to his base to tell him.

Carlos then asked for leave and once he arrived home he didn't want to go back. He had another nine months to complete his service but was too shaken and upset after fifteen months in this battle against the Contra. Mum was afraid he'd be imprisoned for desertion if he didn't return. It was Guillermo, my eldest brother, who sorted this out. Carlos was, in fact, entitled to discharge being Mum's sole provider and that's how he got to stay on at home working in the farming cooperative and on the holding. He couldn't face the fighting any more.

\* \* \*

It feels good knowing Dad is keeping an eye on us. I've taken to heart what he said. I know with time life will get better. When I need him, or he needs me, he comes. The last time Dad came, he sat beside me. Yes, I was asleep and in my dream he said, 'Rosa, wake up please and make me a cup of coffee.' And in my dream I made him a cup. Then he said, 'Now don't go back to sleep.' With that I really did wake up and was getting dressed when there was a knock on the door. It was Guillermo; he'd come to tell me Mum was in hospital. We went straight there. Mum had taken very ill with a kidney infection. I stayed with her, visiting her every day. After two weeks she was well enough to leave and I accompanied her back home.

I feel Dad especially at home in La Concha. It's strange now he's gone how he helps me feel stronger in myself. I went to tell Susana about Rubén. She meant well but when she said, 'Rosa, you'll find another man, you're still young and pretty,' I thought that was the last thing I needed. *Mejor sola que mal acompañada* – better alone than with the wrong man.

The only thing I wish for is to have more time at home with the children but another man wouldn't give me that. That's what I really want and what the children need. It's sad I can't give that and I'm sure it's why Angélica is always asking me for little things. Laura thinks I'm too soft on her. She gets cross with me. 'Why do you always give in to Angélica?' She won't see how Angélica didn't have the same attention as her. Laura has always had Mum for her. Angélica had a hard start in life. She says to me her heart hurts sometimes and asks, 'Why am I like this?' I don't tell her about how it was when she was inside me but I think that tension left her with some problems.

Angélica moved back with me when she started primary school and the house was more comfortable. It's been a big change having electricity brought in and right now we're having extra water taps installed on every block. That'll make life a lot easier. At the moment the nearest water tap is two blocks away and there's always a queue in the morning. The *barrio* Defence Committee has worked hard to have this done. Yes, I'm on the committee: I was asked to represent my end of the *barrio*.

The *barrio* might be rough by some standards but we've no big problems like drugs or prostitution. It's more family matters that crop up, like the five children that were left abandoned. I didn't know their mother but when she died, their dad couldn't cope. A neighbour tried helping and fed them for a while but the dad wasn't contributing. In the end he agreed the only option was for the welfare people to take them. It's a shame, those five children, they went to the children's home.

And another family in trouble is Norma and her two kids. She's staying with me now, but hopefully not much longer. At first I didn't believe her. I thought how could a mother be thrown onto the street? She told me her sister-in-law had stolen her plot, had rigged it with the *barrio* coordinator. You see, Norma had gone away to her parents when her husband died and when she came back she found her home was gone, demolished. So she came to my door looking for help and I took them in.

Norma said she wanted to go to the right-wing newspaper, *La Prensa* – they'd love a story like that – but we managed to sort it out ourselves. I told her we'd go to the Women's Legal Office and to Connie Rosález. Connie was the one who distributed the plots in the first place and when we met with her, she said she'd never come across anything like it.

She came to see for herself and meet with the *barrio* coordinator. She saw to it the plot was given back to Norma. Her house is being rebuilt, hopefully it'll be finished by the end of the week. I should add that this is at the *barrio* committee's expense, not the coordinator's. I'll be glad when she moves. We don't have the space.

The main problem here is the unemployment. A few women have work here in a sewing co-op. But I can see the *barrio* has definitely improved since I moved here six years ago. We've a dining room to see all the kids have at least one decent meal. And a hundred *barrio* kids attend Angélica's primary: fifty in the morning and the other fifty in the afternoon. The two teachers are very dedicated. They're paid by the Ministry of Education. I make the pupils notebooks at work from the paper cut-offs.

\* \* \*

I often think how life would be if it wasn't for the war. Ernesto Tórrez from the *barrio* committee came to tell me a lad had committed suicide, he'd hung himself. Ernesto asked if I'd go and see the boy's mother, Cecilia. She told me her boy had been based in Puerto Cabezas on the Atlantic coast. He'd been wounded by the Contra and had to have his leg amputated. He'd then been sent home and it sounds like he felt life had come to an end; he'd become depressed, stuck at home. She talked a long time. She was in a state of shock. I made a collection towards his funeral. The fighting leaves no escape. This year has been hard.

They see too much, these men. How can they adapt to civilian life? No one can really understand. How can you if you've not gone through what they have? At work there are three like that. They keep to themselves, always busy, always working. One is teaching a literacy class at work, and the quietest one, he's donating his overtime pay to the shop's Rice and Bean Fund. Everyone, though, can feel the pain. Oscar at work, he lost his son, Tomás. He was killed in an ambush. The funeral was held in Ticuantepe, his hometown. I arranged for a group of us from work to go. I didn't know until Oscar told me his son had been fighting in the mountains for five years, since '83. He wasn't a conscript, he was a volunteer and Sandinista militant. We arrived to join the procession and walked behind Oscar and his wife and family. Tomás's battalion carried the coffin. The whole town had turned out. We walked through the main street to the cemetery.

It's Oscar and these other men who've been in the army who are the ones making improvements happen at work. They're the ones keen on having more technical training. Look, from when I started at the print shop, the union has brought in a small clinic and now we're looking to set up a crèche before Christmas. And meals are free at the canteen, and always there's either meat or fish.

Most things we can sort out ourselves, which is just as well. The CST national workers' union headquarters can't respond to small issues. It's caught up dealing with the endless big problems, or trying to. If it wasn't for these economic troubles, I think the country would be way ahead.

* * *

I do say the shop steward training at the CST helped me a lot, especially to sort out the fiddling that was going on at work. The thieving only started with Antonio's arrival. He became director four years ago, in 1984. I don't know why we didn't sniff something wrong then. It seems so obvious now, the way he obstructed the union and dished out loans and favours to the older workers, like lending them the company van, favours to serve as his smoke screen.

The thieving first came to light when Yolanda, the bookkeeper, realized there were major financial discrepancies. She then came to see Frida, the union secretary, and me to discuss this and what to do. She said she was pretty sure it was Dulce, Antonio's secretary, who was on the take. Yolanda showed us how over the years Dulce had taken over more and more control of monies for the welfare, socials and the kitchen, and how she'd managed this, we knew, was by being Antonio's sweetheart.

Next thing, before we could do anything, Dulce got wind of Yolanda's findings and immediately went to Antonio to accuse Yolanda of incompetence. This was to convince Antonio to fire her, which he did. Amazingly, Dulce then thought she was free to up her game. That was when Frida and I went to the union head office with Yolanda. She explained everything she knew but she said she didn't want to fight for her job. The union guy we saw said the CST would look into the matter but, like I said, they were very busy.

Yolanda's bookkeeping post was soon filled by a new woman, Carlotta Moreno. And again, it took Carlotta no time to show how much the company finances were out of order with a lot of money missing. I should add that donated furniture had disappeared too. Antonio kept saying it was in storage but he never said where, and these were donated tools, a fridge, a cooker, furniture and hammocks to be used in the workers' recreation room.

Anyhow, Carlotta's audit left Dulce no way out. With this evidence we thought now was the moment for a full investigation, and our timing was perfect. Antonio was out of the country and the finance officer fired Dulce. It was almost funny, the nerve of Dulce; she went straight to the Labour Ministry to reclaim her job.

When Antonio reappeared, he blew a fuse and refused to sign Carlotta's contract. I thought that was rich. He could only do that since we in the union had negotiated for key jobs to start on a short-term-contract basis to try and control the likes of Dulce. When we asked Antonio his reasoning, he simply said he didn't like the way Carlotta worked, which we reckoned wasn't quite good enough so she took her case to the Labour Ministry claiming unfair dismissal. While they evaluated her case we saw she was kept on full pay and meanwhile Antonio went about the shop like everything was fine. I expect he thought his position would protect him. He's such an operator. He knows what strings to pull in the Sandinista Party.

Carlotta's audit had been sent to the union's head office to be examined together with a survey we did of what the workers wanted. Some had asked for training to be able to do more than one job; others said the wages were way too low, which they are. The key thing was many were showing more interest in how the place could run. That's what I thought anyway.

At last the day came for the shop general assembly to discuss the embezzlement and decide what needed to change. It felt like we had the CST with us now because they'd sent their industrial relations expert in to chair the meeting. All the workers were there in the canteen. Antonio stood up first and talked about anything and everything but the matter in hand, ending his very long speech by heaping praise on the 'dedicated workers'. Then Frida took the floor and gave a detailed breakdown of everything that had gone on, right up to Carlotta's dismissal, which of course showed up Antonio to be at best incompetent and at worst corrupt. The meeting was then opened for questions. I was at the back and thought it best to leave this to others, given how involved I'd already been. It was their time to take the initiative.

*Antonio was at best incompetent and at worst corrupt*

But no one spoke, not one single person, even those I knew were angry about all this, like Oscar. It was dreadful. No one asked a single question, like how come the accounts had got into such a mess, or the pilfering, or where the donations for the recreation room were, never mind how unfair some of the wages are. It was the exact moment to get the boss sacked, but they let slip this golden opportunity.

They don't believe in themselves, in their own power. I felt dreadful, especially when I saw Oscar, just sitting there, asking nothing. Even if everyone is feeling worn out, this was sad, and it annoyed me seeing too the older workers there, knowing how they grab anything that's going – bonuses, time off and new overalls – but are too scared to pick up a pen, never mind their rights.

It ended up looking like the union was victimizing Antonio. The CST representative wound down the meeting asking everyone to work together to improve standards. He also saw to it Carlotta was reinstated, which indirectly was letting the director know, 'no more fiddles'.

The outcome was good insomuch as Antonio now knows he can't ignore us like before. He now shows us the inventory of all incoming materials and there's a new head of finance and welfare who's supervised by the head of administration. Still, we haven't found the missing furniture.

* * *

At least I do still have my job. At the start of this year I was frightened we might be shut down. Antonio told us the electricity cuts were happening too frequently and forcing production to stop-start-stop, so there was no option until the problem was fixed. In a meeting with all the workers Antonio said the closure would only be until the central electricity plant was repaired, which he estimated would take two months. Frida suggested keeping on a skeleton staff like other factories in Managua. Antonio said no to that but promised everyone would keep their jobs and still be paid during this period, which was a huge relief. He then asked if some of us, including me, would come back next day to clean up the place.

The following morning we were there at eight sharp and Antonio walked in. He said he had a surprise for us. We'd been asked to come back not to clean up but to work on a very important secret job. He said we'd been selected because of our commitment, which I thought at least showed he could see in others what he didn't have.

He told us we were going to print posters and leaflets announcing a massive devaluation. The *córdoba*, he said, was to come down from one thousand to the value of one *cordoba*. He went on about what we all knew: how our wages now, in 1988, didn't cover all the basics they once did and how the inflation was out of control. The devaluation, he said, was to contain the profiteering going on and would also leave the Contra inside the country stranded with old currency.

Antonio said this was the tail end of a massive plan that had begun last year. Seemingly thousands of people were involved and they'd all kept it secret. The operation was called 'Martyrs of Quilalí', in memory of the poor women and children massacred by the Contra in the north, in Quilalí.

I hadn't expected to be told that we wouldn't be allowed home until the job was done. Antonio said this was because of the tight deadline but I suspected it was more likely to ensure no hitches, no leaks. We were to sleep and eat in the print shop for three days.

We only had the clothes we were wearing, but more worrying for me was that Darío and Angélica were at home alone. We all had families expecting us and some, like me, had kids on their own.

Antonio suggested we write letters and have the company driver deliver them to our homes, saying only that we had an emergency job and asking for whatever we needed, like clothes, to be sent back. But that wasn't my point. I said, 'My kids can't be left by themselves. What if there's a break-in?' I insisted I go with the driver and I got my way.

When I got home, would you believe it, Mum was there. She'd come from La Concha. Don't ask me how she's always there when I need her. All I could say to her was we had a deadline on a big job. She said she was happy to take the children but of course I knew she thought something was up. I felt bad; she was bound to worry, but imagine if she'd let something slip to Ana about this deflation. Ana would definitely tell her man Lucho, and in no time that would set off panic buying and who knows what. It'd be a disaster.

I got back and started to work on this massive print job. Our only rest was when there were power cuts. I must have slept only a couple of hours in those three days. Security was tight and all dud run-ups were burnt.

We were actually ahead of schedule. Lorries were coming and going to do pick-ups. I kept thinking how incredible it was, this huge operation being kept quiet. And I'd heard on the radio only a few days before that a new five million *córdoba* bill was soon coming into circulation. That was obviously to make out like inflation was just going to go on, up and up.

By the day the job was done, I was exhausted. I fell into bed and slept like a log.

Apart from coffee the house was bare, so when I got up the next morning I went to the Eastern Market. I should have known better since it was the first day of the change of currency. What a hullabaloo! It was a riot, vendors chucking eggs, tomatoes. I saw a woman wielding a machete chasing a price inspector through the market. The sellers were up in arms. 'The government is on the fiddle, fat profiteering bastards.'

This measure, though, did leave the Contra stuck with a lot of old currency. On the radio I heard the Contra had sent a peasant to exchange a load of old *córdobas* in Wiwilí but if you tried to change more than ten million you had to prove where you got that amount, so he was stuck.

The *barrio* committee tried to persuade our local storekeepers to stick to the new official prices and the committee bought cheese direct from a farm in León. But you can't buy everything direct and cut out the middleman, especially if farmers can do better on the open market. Shortages are shortages and the vendors wouldn't keep to the stipulated prices.

The central CST office held a Saturday workshop on how to make efficiency savings in production but within a month I wondered why the government had bothered. This incredible effort to control inflation had failed and prices were again going up so I couldn't afford anything like meat or cheese.

In the first years after the triumph basic foodstuffs like rice, beans and cooking oil were guaranteed at fixed prices and were available. Now our local store hasn't had cooking oil for months.

\* \* \*

With this measure failing I suppose I should have seen what would come next. The government called for major layoffs in the state sector. A third of the workers in all ministries and unprofitable state industries had to go.

They tried softening the blow for these workers by promising jobs outside Managua on the state-owned farms, such as dairy and sugarcane farms, or on the farming cooperatives, at least those supposedly safe from Contra attacks.

They said those folk making the move would have food provided until their first harvest and be given wood and corrugated sheeting to build new homes. I'd call those survival incentives, nothing more.

I'd gone with Frida to a meeting at the CST headquarters to hear more about this from farmers, about how to make the move. They said they'd left Managua after the 1972 earthquake and set themselves up as a farmers' co-op in 1979, after the revolution. They'd come a long way to change life for the better.

I agree the only way out of the crisis is to grow more beans and rice but, personally, I'd need to know if there would be running water, electricity, a school for the children. And if that's my way of thinking, what secretary would opt for a life of grinding maize at the crack of dawn?

I don't know whether it's passivity or exhaustion, but people seem to be accepting these redundancies as inevitable.

I was shocked at Myrna, my brother's girl, how she accepted hers. She'd come with Laura; they both stayed with me. She'd moved here to study and had got this excellent job in the Customs head office to pay for night school. She'd made great strides, studying administration and English.

No, I wasn't happy when Myrna told me she'd taken redundancy voluntarily. Laura told me Myrna wanted to go home to La Concha but when I asked Myrna directly, she made out she didn't want to leave. I told her anyway, 'If you do want to live in La Concha, whatever you do don't give up your job. It'll be impossible to find another like that one'.

That very weekend she was gone. Maybe she hoped her redundancy would carry her through until she found another job.

\* \* \*

I'd love a break but redundancy isn't an option for me. This year has been non-stop work, apart from going to a *fiesta* in the Central Park for Women's Day in March. I took Angélica and Darío and I bought both of them a T-shirt. Marimba bands were playing and we saw a funny play put on by a women's group. We had a good time.

That was only a couple of months ago though feels more like a lifetime ago. Two weeks after that *fiesta* the whole country went into a state of military alert. Reagan sent three thousand US troops into Honduras, where the Contra camps are based. When we heard US troops had arrived in Honduras, the Sandinista Army mobilized all the Civil Defence divisions, here and in every other *barrio*, village and town.

I went to see everyone in my sector to check out how they were and what they could do. I don't know how many offered to help, to donate blood at the communal hall. All the food and candles sold out. Men in Civil Defence and the Territorial Militias were getting ready to leave for the border and most I talked to said they thought Reagan had sent the troops to force concessions from the government, but wouldn't dare invade Nicaragua. I really wanted to believe them, that it would be too dangerous and politically damaging for the US. They thought Reagan sent the troops to keep pressure on the government since the Contra are now so weak. They were badly hit in the last big military offensive, Operation Danto. A thousand Contras were reported killed and that forced their leaders to accept talks with the government.

Over these years we've faced one threat after another from the US, fearing a US military intervention, but now maybe Reagan couldn't invade when the world was watching the Sandinista government negotiating for peace with the Contra leaders. It would turn into another Vietnam, but then again, what does the average American know or care? Talking to my workmates, some said the troops would intervene precisely because the Contras were beaten; that Reagan wanted war until the Sandinistas were completely smashed. The situation was so tense.

So, what would you do if in my shoes? Go to an all-night street party? Well, that's what I did. I went with a bunch of pals from the *barrio* to join the best ever send-off. The government delegation was on its way to negotiate an end of the fighting with the Contra. They drove past on their way to Sapoá, on the border with Costa Rica, and there we were, all along the Masaya Highway, waving and dancing with hundreds of others, to salsa bands and fireworks. It made me feel good. We were sending a message of what we are made of.

The following days we were all ears to the radios. On the third day it sounded like there was hope. An agreement was likely. This could be the beginning of the end to the war. The agreement

*Waving and dancing with hundreds of others*

was to come at a price, though, a high price: an amnesty for all the Somoza *Guardia*, those war criminals who were imprisoned. That's who most of the Contra leaders are: Somoza's *Guardia*. They thirst for power. But it had to be.

The talks exposed big divisions in the Contra political leadership and also among their military chiefs. This was mainly between those who were old *Guardia* and the younger peasant leaders. And this left Reagan cornered. This was a political victory over the Contra. Reagan was being faced down; countries all over the world had condemned this threat of US intervention, and this included US Congress people and senators.

The US troops were pulled out. They didn't cross into Nicaragua, or I wouldn't be talking to you now, would I?

## María

I asked Sergio to bring Guillermo home. I had words with him and he promised to drink only the occasional beer.

Guillermo lives in the next village over from La Concha and has done well. Ernesto taught him his trade. He'd have a lot more work if he could stop drinking.

When I was young only older men would drink. Now on my way to church I see lads as young as fourteen drinking in the park. They should be at Mass, not hanging about like that. Only grown men should drink and only during the *fiestas*.

Roberto and I never had problems about this kind of thing. No, we had no disagreements on this or any other matter. He was a good man; he worked all his days to keep us. Roberto was respected. I couldn't tell you the number of friends who came for his wake, and every one brought us bread or sugar. They gave enough money to afford a good class of coffin. I felt more than grateful to them all. I'll always hold this dear. Rosa came home with some of her workmates who knew our family and they presented us with a beautiful wreath.

The pity was Carlos couldn't be home for the funeral. He was in the mountains, doing his military service. Rosa had tried to contact him by radio but he didn't hear the message, so he wasn't here in time. He only learned about his father's death when I sent him a letter. That was hard on him.

\* \* \*

We all worry about our sons and pray they'll be saved from the Contra. All the time Carlos was in military service, I went to church to pray for his safe return. I go to the main church but many have more faith in Saint Antonio and go to his chapel.

*Pray they'll be saved from the Contra*

*Doña Eva found the little statue of the saint in a pool*

Doña Eva found the little statue of the saint in a pool on her way home from Lake Venecia and understood this to be her calling. Over the years many devotees have come to visit the saint in her home and fill the donation plates with silver. Every year she celebrated the Saint's Day with a *fiesta* and every year more and more devotees came, and this way she could afford to build the saint his chapel.

Padre Ignacio was of the opinion that Saint Antonio should be in the main church to be with the other saints. He had become concerned by the number of followers visiting the chapel. I know he told Doña Eva, 'At your convenience I will offer to say Mass to Saint Antonio when he is in his rightful home.'

She thought the saint belonged to her family and refused to obey the priest. Padre Ignacio was left then in the unfortunate position of having to arrange for the statue to be brought to the church without her consent. But within three days the saint had disappeared off its new plinth in the church and found its way back to the chapel. I heard Eva had said he had returned to his chapel through his miraculous powers.

Soon after his reappearance in the chapel we heard the sad news that Padre Ignacio had had an accident. His horse had dropped dead from under him on his way to Masaya. It was quite wrong of Doña Eva to say this was the saint's retribution. Why would Saint Antonio punish Padre Ignacio? I advise you take care regarding Doña Eva. Saint Antonio should be in the main church.

My mother was a faithful devotee to the saint. Every week she went to pray for my brother's salvation. She stitched the finest piece of embroidery and laid it on the saint's altar. Where it went I'll never know. Doña Eva hasn't even had benches made for the devotees. Padre had good reason to be concerned. He was upholding all aspects of the Church. Saint Antonio is the only saint not housed in the main church.

There was talk when I was young of a saint, a living one, near here, in Masatepe. Mother went to see for herself. She came home and said she wasn't at all convinced and would like my opinion. So the next week I went to where this saint lived. A few others were there when I arrived and we were invited by the saint's father to see her.

She was lying on a bed surrounded by flowers and candles. To me she did look saintly with her long hands and feet and she was alive; I could see her breathing and she appeared asleep.

Her father said her soul had been weighed down by the grief of the world and this was why no one could lift her. He said anyone wishing to know the truth of this was welcome to try, and five men did try. They got around and tried to raise the bed but they couldn't. I came home none the wiser.

Over the next months word spread of the miraculous saint weighed down by the world's sorrow and folk visited from all around the district of Masatepe bringing her offerings. This was until we heard she had 'risen' of her own accord. She'd walked off with her boyfriend, their pockets lined with silver.

In Mass that following Sunday Padre Ignacio made his contempt clear. He would deal very firmly with all immoral people wherever he found them. On his visits to the parishioners he was known for marrying any couples he found living out of wedlock. He would marry them there and then, in their home.

And he made certain all Saints' Days were properly observed. He gave my family the honour of being guardian of the Virgin of Carmen. I still look after her dress at home. This is the best place for her dress for the time being.

Padre Ignacio would delegate a different patron every year to host the Fiesta of the Child of María and one year he requested this of my parents. Preparations had to begin months in advance. Friends and neighbours came with any scraps they had to help fatten up the pig and gave us maize and sugarcane for the sweetcorn biscuits. We were cooking for weeks. Father went to Managua and came home in a truck filled with cassava, plantains and baskets of tomatoes and onions. This was to make the *nacata-males*. We set out the tables on the back patio to prepare three hundred of them. We had to borrow more cauldrons to cook the pork with maize, with mint, chili and cornmeal, and each one we wrapped up in a banana leaf.

*All Saints' Days were properly observed*

The evening before the big day mother and I spent collecting flowers to decorate the shrine for the Child of María in the house. When we'd laid out all the food and drink, everything was ready for the *fiesta*.

From early next day folk came by to visit. They came all day long and we had food and drink enough for everyone, for every child and every grownup to have their fill. And when evening fell the whole town gathered outside in a long procession down the street, ready to start walking behind the bearers to carry the Child of María back to the church and there hear our Padre Ignacio say Mass.

\* \* \*

Padre Ignacio was a visionary. He was the priest who was behind the whole plan for our church to be built. He had it built where the old church had stood. Don Antonio and Don Rodríguez oversaw its building. They went first to Doña Julia. She is a good Catholic lady, of the Carrión family, and she agreed for her finest trees to be felled and her neighbours to lend their oxen to bring the trunks into town. Then Padre Ignacio asked my uncle and other gentleman carpenters to work on their free days to saw the wood and us church women brought them coffee and *chicha*.

When the time then came for the church frame to be raised, Padre held a *fiesta* with marimba music and many more men then offered their labour for the following week.

We were there to see this: Don Antonio and Don Rodríguez calling out, telling the men how to erect the great timber frame into place and raise the sixteen wooden pillars. The pillars are carved out of those same trees donated by Doña Julia.

For the construction of the walls Padre Ignacio held an even grander *fiesta,* for now more men were needed to dig out a new road to reach the stone that was to be quarried. Over the next months and years the men toiled to cut each block and bring them in by oxen.

The church took all of ten years to complete. It was Easter when finally the church opened its doors for the first time. This was the greatest celebration the town ever had. Everyone had been busy in preparation, taking cartloads of feed for the animals and the women cooking enough food for the seven days. Then every kitchen fire was put out and everyone stopped working for the week.

The Easter week began with all the town's folk gathering behind the twelve apostles. They were twelve good youngsters selected by the priest to have this special privilege and lead everyone to our new house of worship and hear Padre Ignacio say Mass.

After Mass everyone came out to join us in the square and there we served *chicha*, fruit juice and corn biscuits. Yes, we ladies of the church served everyone on that great day.

Every day was another celebration. On the Wednesday the older boys led another procession to the church and on the Thursday we went to church to see our Padre Ignacio kneel and wash the feet of these boys. Those words he read from the Bible I know by heart: 'Now that I, your Lord and Teacher, have washed your feet, you also should wash one another's feet. Very truly I tell you, no servant is greater than his master, nor is a messenger greater than the one who sent him.'

The most wonderful of all was the Last Supper and that year this supper was our privilege to prepare. We brought from home the whole supper to serve the twelve apostles and their helpers in the church. We'd cooked a special dish of fish with a cheese, squash and potato sauce, and for their dessert we served them a honey vanilla dessert on small china plates we'd borrowed for the occasion. That night was truly beautiful.

Padre had made an arrangement with the *Guardia Nacional* to borrow their uniforms and rifles for the night. Four churchmen then dressed up as soldiers and carried the statue of Christ from the church to the town's police cell and there they kept watch until dawn.

The next morning we were awake early to walk beyond Barrio Veracruz to where Christ was, on the Cross. All the town folk were gathered there, on the hillside, and we saw Padre Ignacio kneel before Christ. When he rose, he turned to us to hold Mass. And then he spoke the last words Christ ever said. 'Father, forgive them for they know not what they do.' Every precious word Padre Ignacio said with tears in his eyes.

The apostles then brought Christ down from the Cross. Our priest instructed them in every detail. 'Now bring down the left side. Now bring down the right.' And he made sure they did not touch Christ with their bare hands; they had to cover them with little towels. When they took out the last nail, they carefully carried Christ to the church and we all followed on behind.

Every Easter was celebrated like this with Padre Ignacio seeing this happened perfectly.

He served our church for thirty years. He came here every week on horseback from his home in Masaya. He was well acquainted with the family and on occasions we would be invited to visit him in Masaya.

God has received him within His Realm. He has been gone twenty years now. Padre Ignacio dedicated his life to helping others and he died without a *peso*. He had given everything to the Church.

Padre Ignacio was a visionary of prophecies. I don't believe the new priest has this gift and for reasons best known to himself, he has chosen to do away with much of the precious work of Padre Ignacio. He has no interest in how we rejoiced in the Resurrection with the apostles. Us ladies of the church used to meet every month to see everything was in place for all the Saints' Days. He seems reserved about who he will talk to and holds private meetings. Now there's a secretary to book your Mass.

His main interest is with his new Delegates of the Word: youngsters he sends to find couples he can marry in collective wedding services. In truth, I don't know why he has changed so much. But then I can't be saying I don't have time for this priest. I am Catholic and will always be, whoever our priest is.

# 3 In the heart

*It is 1990 and there is a general election in Nicaragua. Mounting economic problems, the unpopular conscription law, and the losses and destruction caused by the Contra war have all sapped support for the Sandinistas.*

## Rosa

I got up early to go vote and then went to help on the electoral table, ticking off the names of the people voting.

People were waiting in line for two blocks. I reckon everyone in our *barrio* must have voted and if that was anything to go by, then the Sandinistas had won.

That's what I thought, up until ten o'clock that night.

Then it became clear the Sandinistas were losing.

I couldn't believe it. Everything felt like it was slipping away from under me. I didn't sleep all that night for worrying about what would happen. All I could see was how everything we'd worked and fought for was going to be destroyed and we'd be back to how things were under Somoza. I also thought about how I'd probably be sacked and the print shop sold.

The next morning was grey, overcast. It felt like a National Day of Mourning. I can't say how long I sat at home. I sat there until I couldn't stand it anymore and went walking along the main road. There wasn't a car to be seen. I then wandered through the *barrio* and everyone I spoke to said the result must be a lie, it must be fraud, it's not like they say it is. But I knew the elections had been clean; there'd been no fraud.

I came home and switched on the radio. People were being interviewed and saying what they thought had happened. The station is just up the road so I thought why not go too? I jotted down a few notes and went there with five of my neighbours. When I explained why I'd come I was taken through to a studio.

The guy running the show asked what I thought and there I was, talking live. I said something like this: 'The Sandinistas ran the cleanest elections in the country's history, and lost to a party that was backed to the hilt by the United States of America. People voted for the UNO coalition using their freedom of choice. These 1990 elections were clean elections and everyone knows this would never have happened under Somoza. Everyone knows Somoza won by fraud.'

I went on about how I'd grown up under the dictator and I woke up in those times, 'so no one is going to tell me that our new UNO president, Doña Violeta, is committed to the people. She'll never win over those who worked for this revolution. After serving her class of people for all those years, I know her type of politics all too well and if she's planning on taking us back to those dark days, she better think again. She'll be met by the full force of the people.' I said this and it went out live.

I walked to work the next day to try and calm down. Everyone was talking about the elections. It was obvious I'd been crying and my old workmate Oscar put his arm around me and said, 'Good on you for telling Doña Violeta where she stands.' He'd actually recorded the programme and played it back. We had to laugh. It came across so strong. We talked about the results and it was a consolation knowing the Sandinistas were still the biggest party. We had forty-one per cent of the vote while the fourteen parties that made up UNO meant not one of them would have had a chance of winning if they'd gone it alone.

I don't think UNO expected to win because they had no electoral celebration to speak of. They tried something last-minute in the Plaza of the Revolution but by ten at night it had fizzled out.

Instead they held a private do in the Intercontinental Hotel. And here in the *barrio* Violeta's supporters got drunk in the community hall, which only ended when they tried to set the place on fire.

Yes, for the past six months since Violeta took office UNO has done absolutely nothing here. It's us from the original *barrio* committee still doing all the work. Rigoberta was telling me she'd gone to the last UNO meeting here and it was a shambles, with them squabbling about how they had no help. It's a reflection on UNO's split between President Violeta and her Vice President, Virgilio Godoy. Their only joint action we've seen in Managua was the painting over of the lovely wall murals because they'd been all about the revolution.

It's as I feared. We're left to fend for ourselves against what is like a never-ending hurricane. The electoral promises have come to nothing. I thought at least the new currency, the *córdoba oro*, might stabilize prices. UNO is forcing layoffs everywhere and you should see the market now; it's bursting with unemployed doctors, teachers, nurses, all trying to sell a bit of something to make a living. We've more vendors than buyers. Vendors are going to Honduras to buy crates of Coca-Cola to sell here.

It's because no one's investing. And where are all the promised foreign donations?

What a joke, UNO's slogan: 'Working together for the good of all'. Instead, everyone's looking out for *Número Uno*, Number One. Before UNO came to power life was tough but we coped because we helped each other. We had to. Look how prepared we were for Hurricane Joan. That was only two years ago, in October 1988. The Sandinista government made sure every school closed, saw that the Civil Defence and Red Cross had medical support in every *barrio* and as a result, we would have survived fine if the hurricane had actually crossed into Managua. Those most at risk, the elderly and mums with babies and kids, were moved to the church and we had milk, coffee and bread to share out. Rigoberta's husband, he came over and secured my roof. Everyone was weighing down their roof with tires and stones. Buckets were topped up and candles bought before the water and electricity were cut off, and then we waited.

The hurricane pretty much petered out by the time it got here. The full force was felt instead on the Atlantic side. The town of Bluefields was flattened, devastated, and those poor people there, thousands were left homeless. All the clothes, shoes, everything we collected was sent there, to the coast. Then the emergency aid started to arrive, first from Cuba, then Sweden, Mexico and Germany, but nothing from the US government.

Five men from the print shop volunteered to go and help build new homes. They were away for three months and when they came back they told us how bad it was.

But what I'm saying is that because we were so well prepared and organized, we got through that crisis.

Rigoberta and I, we've talked a lot about the elections. I think we lost mainly because Daniel Ortega couldn't end the military draft. On the radio I was listening to some soldiers saying how Ortega had forced them to fight. It wasn't him; the war was forced on us. He didn't want any youngsters fighting. There was no choice because the US kept the war going and we couldn't go on and on hoping the Contra would accept peace.

The peace negotiations were still going on right up to the elections. The Sapoá peace negotiations in 1988 hadn't stopped the fighting. The Contra violated the ceasefire. Their top chiefs had too much at stake; the war was big business for them. They were scrabbling over the last of the US funding; that's what kept the

*We were so well prepared and organized, we got through that crisis*

war going all those years. People voted not so much against the Sandinistas but for no more bloodshed.

That's why we had to have the draft. The US paid Somoza's old *Guardia* to fight us and paid for their military bases in Honduras. Without the US the Contra war could never have happened. We had to fight and then when we were near to winning, Reagan threatened full-scale intervention.

The Contra couldn't have come into being without the CIA. They paid people who'd never been part of the Sandinista struggle but they weren't all the old Somoza *Guardia*. The Contra soldiers were mostly civilians who didn't believe in the aims of the revolution or didn't understand them. It was the CIA who bought them with dollars. My understanding is that's how they were recruited, and others were kidnapped. Most of the foot soldiers came from the north and Atlantic side of the country.

The United States has always used us like its backyard and couldn't take it when we went our own way. I'm clear about this. They had to destroy us because we were showing it could be done, to be independent and do what was best for the people. It's true, we held a flame alight in the heart of Latin America. They needed to kill off the hope we gave the poor of Latin America.

How many times has the US threatened to invade us? And the Contra did its work for it. The US never let up and it used our weak spots. And on top of this fighting and so many natural disasters, it strangled us with its economic blockade. The shortages affected everyone – the lack of oil, sugar, soap – and it all got to be too much.

But why didn't I see the election defeat coming? I was sure we'd keep on going, that the Contra would finally be defeated, and I believed most of my workmates thought the same. I kept thinking this even when only five workers, six including me, had volunteered to help on the elections. They'd say things like, 'Violeta Chamorro, she'll never be president. She's got no political experience.' And I believed Amalia meant what she said, 'We're bound to win what with the military, teachers, health workers and poor folk all voting Sandinista.' She was a pal at work, active in the women's organization, AMNLAE, and a volunteer in a women's battalion. Then two days after the elections she told me, 'I'm sorry, Rosa, all I could think about was my son, that he'd be conscripted. I was so frightened, I voted UNO.'

I can't blame her. I haven't wanted to tell you this: you know Susana, my friend from way back when I was with Federico and Inés? She lost her boy Alfredo. He was killed by the Contra in Pantasma, along with fifteen other soldiers. He was sixteen and had only been in the army three months. He'd followed his older brother Uriel, who had been fighting five years. Alfredo gave up school to go. He was a very clever boy.

Susana just broke here inside and I don't think she'll ever recover from this blow. It's been hard watching her working and working, all hours, doing what she always did for AMNLAE. She needs to hold on to her love for the revolution. She's got great strength but I know she was keeping busy to distract herself. Anytime I called on her, she was on her way out to visit coffee pickers or a women's collective. She has a way that draws people. It's because she respects everyone. I joined her on an outing with a group of prostitutes and I could see how these women really took to her. We visited a group of women running their own shoe co-op in Masaya. We then went on to León to meet women there who'd been prostitutes themselves. They were making cheese and other milk products and also bricks. That was about a year ago. Susana was offering alternatives.

She had to leave her job with AMNLAE when the funding dried up. She's now in the Eastern Market selling clothes and joined the stall sellers' committee there to try and keep control on the rents. Her other lad, Uriel, lends her a hand. He's a bus driver and gives her some money. I really feel for her. I see her when I can.

\* \* \*

It was only after the Sandinista defeat that I could stand back and began to see beyond the war and the shortages. I began thinking about the attitudes and expectations of folk at the print shop. It struck me how the women at work wanted a nursery built, but it

89

was always, 'Who'll fundraise, who'll buy the building materials, who'll build it?' It was always someone else, me and Frida, who were left doing the running. So who went to the Fanatex factory last year to get ideas for the nursery? Me. And there I could see the Fanatex women weren't like that. They'd worked for free to set up their nursery and they'd made the cots and furniture themselves. We weren't like those women and I was worn out. My doctor had spelt it out. 'Keep going like this and you can expect heart failure.'

So instead of being given the push, I pushed myself. After eleven years, I resigned. I quit in 1990 right after the elections. I'd already packed in my union work. Frida and I couldn't cope with the new management. And the shop stewards were useless, sitting back while management fired one worker after another. Frida and I couldn't fight on alone.

When I handed in my notice, I was really touched and surprised by the generous send-off. It was a weekend holiday at the seaside resort with all my family in El Valero. We left Friday and came back on the Sunday. Mum, Myrna, Laura, Angélica and Darío all came, along with fifteen workmates and their families. We had beautiful beach houses to sleep in and ate breakfast in the restaurant, all paid for. I'd never been there and it was great.

\* \* \*

I had to go but leaving was hard. I couldn't keep going. Like so many women, I hadn't just worked a double day; I'd worked a triple day. I was mum and dad, a full-time worker, and a union shop steward and *barrio* coordinator. I look so old for my age – I'm no advert for this better life we wanted. For years I've been up at four in the morning to collect water, wash clothes, cook breakfast, then seen the kids off to school, and after a full day's work gone to a *barrio* meeting.

I was thinking about the women like me who'd given so much for the revolution. It's daft how I felt personally responsible for the Sandinista defeat. I kept thinking, if only the union had been able to offer more incentives to the workers, especially women, to study or train to operate the machines. The union wasn't strong enough and for all my requests to AMNLAE and the CST to run study circles, I'd not even gotten a reply.

Over the years I saw how it became more like, 'I'll scratch your back if you scratch mine'. Why some were awarded Sandinista Party Militant I'll never know. We had one at work, and once he was awarded he thought himself way above the rest of us and was never there when needed. And how else did the mayor's sister in La Concha get her job as the council's secretary? I saw how the Sandinista leaders had distanced themselves over the years.

Maybe I had wanted to turn a blind eye. I hadn't a clue at the time about the *piñata*. It happened in the three months before Violeta Chamorro was inaugurated. They called it the *piñata* because it was just like a party only with a lot of 'big kids' grabbing everything they could, emptying warehouses, clearing out everything from the ministries.

I only found out later that when I left my job, the management went straight in there with its own *piñata*. The director and top administration met in private, then they told the rest of the personnel the business was no longer viable, that they'd be moving to smaller premises with a reduced staff. That way they closed the print works. Oscar told me he knew of a few small print shops that had got going with staff from work, using the shop's equipment.

Meanwhile I'd seen no severance pay, and it would have been a fair amount. Before I left, I'd been promised this would be sorted out and told to meet with management, but the Monday meeting never happened, nor the following Tuesday's or the next Monday's.

I gave up in the end and when I finally got around to seeing the CST about it, I was told the print shop no longer existed. I checked this out with Oscar. He said one of the managers had left for the States, another for Guatemala, and there was no management left to talk to. I'd been robbed for all those years of work.

I could understand those who said, 'Why leave everything for UNO and their cronies to have their own *piñata*?' At least in those three transition months the Sandinistas pushed through laws to legalize all the housing and land they'd given folk during the revolution. And I know more land takeovers happened during that time.

But what I'm asking is why my boss, Antonio, got a mansion of a house? And Ernesto Tórrez, he made a killing. To think I'd once respected him. The *piñata* set him up nicely, making concrete blocks in his so-called cooperative. He'd started out with ten men telling them, 'This cooperative belongs to all of us and we'll be able to provide the *barrio* with low-cost building materials.' As soon as he'd filled his yard with materials from the Construction Ministry, all for free, and was going at full capacity, he cut out the associates. And how many top union leaders now have farms, men who started out with nothing, workers like the rest of us?

* * *

I had hopes at least the fighting would end with the masses of soldiers being discharged from the army but many, after never receiving their promise of land and redundancies, refused to hand in their weapons. And they know as well that the top brass made out just fine with houses, farms and dollars. UNO even cut the War Wounded Benefit just at the time when thousands of soldiers and Contras were demobilized. Many have returned to the mountains, and I'm talking about both Sandinista soldiers and Contras. You read this in the papers, the 'Re-Contra' are again attacking farming cooperatives in Nueva Guinea, Wiwilí and Nueva Segovia, and the coffee again isn't being picked. There's a good coffee crop in Río Blanco going to rot. And there's the Church preaching reconciliation and forgiveness and working together. Like I say, it's like an earthquake ripping the country apart. When the pension for the Mothers of Heroes and Martyrs was cut, Susana was in tears. I went on the radio again to speak out against it. I should have stayed on the air because UNO then laid off a hundred workers from the municipal government. Next came a mass dismissal from the state telecommunications company followed by staff from the state electricity utility, then workers in the state textile and metal factories. UNO then began destroying the agrarian reform, our hard-won right to land. How can the government justify these measures now that the US blockade and war are over?

The response wasn't long in coming. The first strike was a month after Violeta's inauguration. But UNO wasn't negotiating and by July it was clear there was nothing to lose.

First one factory, then two, then ten went out on strike and when the Transport Ministry joined, that was the signal for everyone to come onto the streets.

Barricades went up across Managua blocking all the main streets; it was almost like 1979. The whole city came out, everyone doing what they could. I took bread and coffee to the Fanatex workers occupying their factory. The women in the textile factories are facing three hundred to be laid off and how come, when they're working three shifts day and night to meet their export order? The government can't say they're not profitable. Like I said, I'd been there last year, before the elections, for ideas about our crèche so I know some women there.

Vice President Godoy has sent in a mob of ex-Contras he calls the Brigade for National Salvation to break up the strike and the UNO labour minister sent in his own thugs. Two strikers were killed.

Doña Violeta went on waving her big stick, sending police to the factories along the Northern Highway, but they wouldn't attack the strikers because their allegiance isn't with UNO.

UNO made out Daniel Ortega was behind the strike but he wasn't the one building all those barricades. In an interview on

*I took bread and coffee to the Fanatex workers*

TV he said the Sandinistas didn't hold the elections to seize back power this way. It took the country to come to a standstill before UNO would negotiate. The strike had spread to all the major towns and cities.

The National workers union has made it clear it doesn't want another strike but I think we're heading for further clashes. There's been unrest even in La Concha.

I'm spending my time at home, making ice in my fridge to sell and making some clothes to order. That just gets us by and Laura chips in too. Darío also helps any way he can. He's grown up a lot in the last year. He's fifteen now and has come on in his arithmetic and reading. His teacher says he'll make a good carpenter. He needs to be able to fend for himself. I don't want him dependent on Laura or Angélica.

He's gained a lot in confidence. At the street carnival he forgot all about us as soon as he met his mates from school. Off he went on one of the floats. The street carnival was Los Pipitos' Third Anniversary. Los Pipitos is for children with disabilities and they work with the parents, teaching them how best to care for their children. Its president is Roberto Espinoza, who has a child with disabilities. It's planning to open centres around the country including one for Jinotepe, near La Concha. It's an excellent charity. They should be state funded.

I worry more about Angélica and her schooling. This supposedly 'new' education programme promoted by the US I'd say is thirty years out of date. It's more like, 'out with the *new* and in with the *old*'. Angélica's teacher was fired purely because she's a Sandinista. The teacher's union is fighting back but it's up against too much of this kind of thing and can't cope.

# 4 Wild grass

*It is 1994 and four years since the Sandinistas lost power. Their supporters are starting to recover from the shock, but there are few jobs, public spending has been slashed, and Rosa and others are turning their energy to organizing in the community.*

## Rosa

I was doing all those jobs I'd never got around to, cleaning the patio, gardening. And after I'd put up a couple of panels to make another room I pulled out a box from under the bed, the one where I kept my personal papers.

'Why keep all this stuff?' I thought and set the lot alight – union papers, AMNLAE leaflets. I was feeling angry. All that work I'd done and for what? And at what cost to my children? I was thinking how I'd neglected them for this revolution and it was all too late now.

I don't know why it didn't click, but my social security card was in among these papers. And pay records. It was Angélica who said, 'Hang on, you need those papers. You could be entitled to social security benefits.' She was right. I received no severance pay but I was still eligible for social security for all the years I'd worked, and we needed every *córdoba* I could get.

Rigoberta said she'd go with me to the Social Security office. When we were finally seen the woman said I needed my ID card, which had also gone up in smoke. I also needed it to get another job. It's a passport to work, making references less important. What a bother. Getting my ID card renewed meant finding my birth certificate, which luckily I still had; it was in another safe place I have in the cupboard. I pulled it out of the folder and then it dawned on me: my name on the certificate is

María, not Rosa. I'd forgotten all about that. You see, Mum had wanted me to have her name, María, and registered me as that at birth. It was my godmother who thought Rosamaría was a nicer name and Mum agreed so asked the priest to christen me Rosamaría. But from then on everyone called me Rosa, never Rosamaría. I was always Rosa and was registered from there on as that.

I was told it would take a year to change my birth certificate. I'd have to pay a lawyer to do this and with no job I had no money, and with no ID no job, and with no lawyer no ID, and with no ID no social security pay either.

Oh well, there were no jobs going anyway. I went on making ice and sewing clothes. I had nowhere to go and no interest in anything. Sometimes I went to a *barrio* meeting and picked up that the FSLN was now listening to its members but what did I care? The only visitors I had were Rigoberta and Julio from the old *barrio* committee, who'd drop by for a chat sometimes. I was tired and bored.

On one of his visits Julio told me about a new community kitchen being set up in the *barrio*. He asked if I and Rigoberta might be interested in helping. Julio said it was being set up to feed the poorer kids. The old one had long since lost its funding. He suggested we visit a Sister Lupita, who was coordinating the project, so I did, and I liked what she had to say. She explained that the idea was for a soya bakery and kitchen. She said it would be collective and non-profit. It shows how out of touch I was. I hadn't heard anything about these Mexican nuns. Sister Lupita was looking for around twenty women to run the project and cook with soya beans. She said the soya milk and food would be for pregnant women, breastfeeding mums and children from zero to ten years old.

It had a name: 'SoyaNica'. She said a few women had already signed up, and there and then I did too. I knew most of the women she mentioned and realized they'd all lost someone in the war or were by themselves, living alone. I suggested I could approach Cecilia, the woman whose son had committed suicide after he'd lost a leg in the war.

The next day I went and knocked on her door and she invited me in for coffee but the moment I asked if she might be interested in the project, she said, 'Why do you think I'd want to help? I want nothing, nothing but to see my son alive again.'

'I'm sorry. I only came because I thought you might be interested. I've been stuck at home all year planting flowers, and for what? To watch them grow? I need something else, something

*I've been stuck at home all year planting flowers*

else to grow. I'm sorry. I know no one can undo what happened. But for the kids' sake, what else is there?' I should have gone about this a different way. I said that and left.

But you know, she did come along! And she in turn approached Thelma. Thelma's daughter had been in the army. Thelma never saw her again and never found out what happened. Thelma's in her sixties, and she was drinking to forget.

It was us women who cleared the yard in the community centre to make space for the brick oven. The kitchen's much bigger now, we have gas stoves too and are running at full capacity. We're nearly forty women keeping the kitchen going to feed over eighty children. We make soya burgers, soup and milk. There'll always be another mouth to feed. Next year we should be up to feeding two hundred. These kids, they sell newspapers, clean car windows, beg. There are hundreds more needing a decent meal.

We just did our first evaluation. I started when the project began in 1991 and Sister Lupita drew SoyaNica like it was a small sapling, to show us when we came together to learn how to cook soya to make it tasty and to learn about its nutritional value. Then she drew a trunk with two branches to show what we'd become by 1992, with the kitchen and the sewing group; then she added three more branches for the youth club, the weaving group and the medicinal gardens we have now. We all said what a lot we'd achieved in these three years.

The herbal medicinal garden was an idea of mine. With the *barrio* health clinic now closed, we really need these remedies. The plants are coming on nicely. Darío has taken on watering them; he likes gardening. Before we started this I went on a short course with two of us SoyaNica women. I knew some cures from Mum but learned a load more and we also learned how to massage, practising together, doing it together and that was something new and very enjoyable.

We're always having other community groups coming here to see what we do and wanting ideas on what medicinal plants to grow. There's real interest out there. Our natural medicine clinic should pay for itself.

We do all this work voluntarily and are given rice, beans and soap each month in compensation by the project's charity. But this isn't enough, nor is selling ice. I make a bit more doing the weekly ironing for the Solís family. The other ladies in the project try and make ends meet selling *tortillas* and sweets, so some days we're down to three women cooking in the kitchen. Somehow it always works out and you can see we've become a magnet for the *barrio*.

*Working together has pulled me out of my depression*

Working together in the project has given me strength, pulled me out of my depression. I think I can say that's probably true for all of us.

It's been great getting to know other women too; I'm talking about women from other parts of the country. We had this big get-together when SoyaNica invited women from communities as far away as Quilalí. They were invited to come see what we were doing and share their experiences.

One woman I spoke to, Katia, a real tough lady, a bit older than me, she'd come all the way from Wiwilí from a farm co-op there. It'd taken her two days to get here. She said she was only now learning to read and write but she knew all about delivering babies. She'd been properly trained during the eighties and they'd built a health clinic but now, for lack of government funding, it was closed. That didn't stop babies being born, she said, and she just went whenever called upon.

And another lady from Estelí, she is a member of a brick factory and bakery co-op and the income they generate is enough to run a women's shelter, one there and another in a nearby town.

This gathering made it much clearer what we're doing and why. There were women from way north, Ocotal, who talked about their work with farmers in San Limay, showing them how they could use their soya to make milk, bread and soup, like we do.

'Peasant to Peasant' is a network that's all about spreading traditional knowhow about what grows best and in which type of soil, which goes to reduce costs. And they grow the soya alongside sorghum, which allows less use of insecticide.

We were together three days. The first workshop was to discuss how we thought we'd been conditioned, thinking about this back from when we were girls. Like one woman said, 'When I was five I was given a broom and I've been sweeping ever

101

since.' We were all saying the same kind of thing so it wasn't embarrassing talking about our bodies either. I'd never done that before, spoken about private matters like that. Most of us had no idea what was happening when our first period came, never mind how we got pregnant. Everyone agreed we thought young women were less inhibited these days. Angélica knows all about sex and is more confident about, say, playing volleyball, but we also thought plenty of them still saw themselves as second to men.

The next day we talked about women's expectations. I think most of us saw that this depended on class; I mean a professional woman can afford to have a maid to mind her baby and can ensure the baby grows into a healthy child, but a woman out in the rural areas or here in the *barrio*, she's up before dawn to light a fire to make the *tortillas* and coffee, then she has to feed the kids. Her life is more about survival, like it is for most of us.

The last workshop had us really fired up. We were discussing, 'What do we want?' Everyone agreed that to start off we had to know how to read and write. We were really talking about how important it is to feel confident, which tied in with what we'd talked about in the first workshop, about knowing ourselves and taking pride in ourselves, and wanting more control over our lives. And this led on to how we go about representing our community. We all knew we were setting an example by how we conducted ourselves, and being honest in every way was the reason we were trusted. I told them about a pregnant girl who has come twice looking for our help and needing us to go with her to the Ixchen Clinic. That's a mobile women's clinic that provides sex education and counselling. The girl is disabled and she couldn't cope. No one wants to have an abortion, but she had no option and here it's illegal. It should be legal.

Everyone said how much they'd got out of coming and I was so sorry to see them leave. This networking is the way to go. I couldn't believe we'd only been together three days. It was like we'd known each other forever. We'd all become friends and discovered we'd so much in common. These women made me feel stronger. All of us were involved either in health care, education or some kind of need in our communities. We can't fill the gaps that opened up after the Sandinista government defeat, but our different initiatives have taken root because they're needed. It's all about being constant and loving and that's what has made everything we've done so far grow, I mean the work in the *barrio*, the community centre, the soya project, the family psychological service, all of it. This kind of work in the *barrios* I see is spreading like wild grass.

Our get-together just shows how many women have moved on. I do think there's more respect nowadays between men and women; men like my brother Carlos, he'll do his share of washing, helping with what needs doing.

Of course I know there's the flip side: domestic violence is definitely getting worse. We'd talked about this in the workshops, about how women challenging their traditional roles can positively challenge men too, or can threaten them or undermine them, especially when they're without a job.

I thought about this afterwards. I mean if this was the first time I'd spoken with so many women about important things, then obviously men would benefit too, but you don't see men discussing personal things, like their conditioning or their role in the community. How could that happen? Take my daughter Laura's husband, Heraldo; I can't see him doing that. He's a nice enough guy but I have to say he makes Laura look foolish. 'Laura, my dinner, and I want a fruit juice. And have you ironed my

103

shirt?' Laura married Heraldo and now they have a boy. And the same with her cousin Myrna – it upsets me thinking about her. She has a baby as well. That sort of confirms what I was saying that there's still many women who see themselves as second to their men.

Darío has told me he doesn't like Heraldo staying here; this is his home after all. Heraldo says they'll find somewhere else but I don't see him looking. What they're waiting for I can't say. Rubén and I, we built this home out of what we could afford. But that's not for them. Laura's father, David, actually offered her a house he inherited in San Marcos, which isn't that far from Managua. Imagine turning down a proper house. I feel she still bears him a grudge for not being around when she was young. It's obvious David cares. He was all over her baby when he came to visit. Yes, he's been very generous towards her. It wasn't only me supporting her all these years.

If the *barrio* committee still had the powers it once had, maybe they'd have been in with a chance for a plot. They don't seem to realize what it takes to make a home or, for that matter, to hold onto it. A woman turned up at my door calling herself Amelia Contreras and told me she owned my plot. She came demanding that I pay her a crazy amount and threatening me with eviction if I didn't pay. She kept waving some paper she had in her hand, which could have been anything for all I knew.

Maybe she thought I had no land deed. 'Señora, you're mistaken,' I said. 'This plot was given to me by the Central Barrio Committee of Managua ten years ago and I have the document to prove it.'

'Why you little Sandinista thief,' she said.

'No, lady, like everyone else I have a right to a place to live. Why should I give you money for land you say you left years ago?'

What a blessing I still had my deed. I'd kept it in that same folder with my birth certificate. I didn't know who Amelia Contreras was, but I knew UNO had just changed the housing law. For all I knew I might be evicted even with my deed. This woman had me worried. Evictions were happening everywhere so I went to check it out with the *barrio* committee.

And a good job I did. I was told everyone had to reapply for a renewal of their original land deed, but they had to have their old one to do this. If you had no deed then you could be evicted. It was this or face being homeless. The committee knew reapplying for the whole *barrio* would more likely prove successful than leaving it to each family to try and sort it out themselves, but we had to get moving. We talked to everyone, block by block, sector by sector, to check they all had their deeds. I visited every family in my sector to explain we had to collect their original deeds, along with birth certificates, social security cards and, if they had jobs, proof of place of employment. It was massive what the *barrio* committee did. And then we set off with all these papers carefully collated to make our claim at the Housing Ministry. But when we were seen, well, we were told we were missing something. Each new land deed cost fifty *córdobas*. It was like an endurance test. Back we went to tell every household the news and of course many couldn't afford that and had to borrow. And I forgot to add, each new deed needed a stamp that cost another ten *córdobas*.

So off we went again once we had the money and this time some other residents came too. Ah, wait for it: this time the ministry told us the new land deeds were now being handled by another department which was, yes, on the other side of town.

Two bus journeys later, we found ourselves at the end of a line stretching for more than a block. There were folk from every *barrio* in Managua, everyone in the same boat. The guy in front was saying, 'The mayor wants rid of the lot of us.' And not until we held the new stamped land deeds did I believe we were safe. It totally depended on having proof, evidence. And many don't. Mayor Alemán evicted forty families in Villa Fraternidad, had their homes demolished and then sent in his anti-riot squad. The people fled and had to camp out on open ground they've named Los Milagros, because they say it's a miracle they're still there. I've been to visit them. They're sleeping under roofs of plastic sheeting. I took them some tins of powdered milk the *barrio* committee collected for their babies. They told me they'll not be moved, not until they have somewhere else to go. But we'll see. You won't see any of this on the TV. What you see is Alemán opening a new park he's had laid down on top of these flattened homes. You watch: he'll bulldoze his way into the big chair, the presidency.

\* \* \*

I knew there'd be changes, but not like this. We're riding a truck with busted brakes and it's frightening. Sure, some top Sandinistas had dirt on their hands, but nothing compared to this mayor of Managua. Alemán's thieving is criminal and corruption is rife. He's grabbed the land that had been allocated for the *barrio*'s new school. The plans were for a playing field, everything a school needs, even a library. We had the promise of overseas funding. Alemán is hanging onto the site, for who knows what.

But forget the new school. It's holding onto what we already have that's our worry. The landowner who owns the land where Angélica's school is wants to demolish the school because of its location. We hear she has plans for yet another shopping mall.

The parents have set up the school committee and we have a good lawyer in Señor Mejía. I thought also to approach Dora María Tellez and Mónica Baltodano for support, since they're both honest Sandinista leaders. We sent letters to the teachers' union as well. We've done the initial fundraising with our raffle called 'Save Our Naraja School'. We've been selling these tickets on the streets and buses and had a good response.

This and the *fiesta* last Saturday brought in enough to cover the legal costs so far. It started at eight and was sold out. By the end of the evening we'd even sold out of drinks so I cleaned up the bar and Clara and Leda told me to go, they'd do the rest.

Next morning I went to see Leda. They were both there and in such a state. Leda had a black eye. What happened was, they'd locked up and were walking to Leda's place with the night's takings. Clara said a taxi drew up alongside and two men jumped out so she made a dash for it. With all the shouting a woman opened her door and Clara just threw the bag to her and rushed back to help Leda but the guys drove off with her inside.

Leda was petrified. She said these men opened her bag and when they found nothing they yelled and punched her. She told them she didn't have it and was totally confused when the men told the driver to go to the police station. Yes, they went with her to the station and dragged her in. These hoods then accused Leda of being drunk and starting a fight and they wanted to press charges against her. She could only think they wanted to scare her into telling them where the money was.

Clara rushed back for her bag with all the money then called on her mobile for a pal to come and pick her up, and together they went to report Leda's kidnapping. Clara couldn't believe her eyes. She and her pal walked into the station to find these guys with Leda. She said these hoods then rounded on her with the policeman too. 'And where's the money now?'

'That's none of your business.' She kept cool and said she was going to call our lawyer, Señor Mejía. That's when the two hoods gave the nod and said they wouldn't bother pressing charges and just walked out of the station.

We've spoken with Señor Mejía and he thinks all this was about stopping us campaigning, that the landowner had hired these thugs to intimidate us. And that policeman must have been involved, definitely, and I'll tell you why: Leda went back to the police station to press charges, but another policeman was on the desk and he said no such incident was logged.

'And if I'd been killed, would that have been recorded?' Leda couldn't believe it.

At least the money was saved. *El Nuevo Diario* newspaper covered the story with a photo of Leda. We're not sure that was such a good idea, since the landowner might try it again. Well, we're easy enough to find. It worries me, this kind of thing happening in the *barrio*. The violence here is getting bad. The house four doors down, their girl's a pal of Angélica but I've put a stop to her visits. Their dad is a drug dealer.

I have to keep an eye on Angélica. She's headstrong. I take her to school and she doesn't like that. 'My pals keep asking if there's something the matter with me.' She feels embarrassed but I need to know she's safe in school. Then I wonder what she's learning. Reciting the Commandments and Sacraments and there's no saying no to learning this way. The Church even stopped the education on AIDS the Health Ministry was promoting and supposedly we have AIDS as bad as Mexico and the US.

## Rosa and María

**María:** Come outside. See those holes, up by the roof?

There was no warning. We just fell to the ground. The bullets were flying.

They got away, the men shooting, through the farm at the back. They had their faces masked. I don't think they could have been from here.

I didn't see the wounded. Ana said they were all taken to hospital. We know it was Don Salas, he hired the men. After all these years he's come back. We knew he'd want to evict the families but to do such a terrible thing! These families have nowhere to go. They've been farming that land for over ten years. I hear the union man came to talk to Don Salas. They've reached an agreement for him to get back most of his land, but not all.

**Rosa:** I don't know, giving land back to Don Salas is bad. He should be arrested. This is happening everywhere. You know the trouble we had renewing our land deeds. The rich are back and want to evict us all.

**María:** And here no one can get any farming credit. Marcos hasn't been able to plant this year. And Guillermo hasn't found any building work. The number of young men not working can only lead to taking things that don't belong to them.

Myrna says next door to her they've started up gaming, and it's not only gambling. She says they're dealing drugs to youngsters. I think the parents are at fault.

**Rosa:** Mum, they're not the only ones at fault. Last night when you were at Mass, Marcos's mates passed Mauricio the bottle and to be drinking at his age and with his condition.

**María:** I know, poor Mauricio.

**Rosa:** And does Dora even know?

**María:** Oh, now, leave this to me. Dora did well asking Los Pipitos to send their doctor, a Dr Geraldo Solís. That was three weeks ago and he examined all the children like Mauricio. Dora took him and I went with Flor's girl and we met at the clinic. Dora's hoping Los Pipitos will open one of its centres here. There are certainly enough children with special needs to warrant one. I'd thought there'd be no more than fifteen children attending but there were more like thirty.

**Rosa:** Yes, the one in Jinotepe is too far for Mauricio to travel. Mum, what about Dora? I thought she'd drop by.

**María:** She has a job she needs to finish, alterations. She's so short of cash she's only sending Pilar to school. She's stopped her check-ups too; she's seeing the herbalist instead.

**Rosa:** There are herbs I know that help with her kind of kidney complaint. I can make quite a few remedies now. I've learned what helps with a lot of ailments. You know we've started up a herb garden since the *barrio*'s health clinic closed; it's where folk come now.

**María:** Your grandma would have liked to have seen that. These remedies seem to be making a comeback. The new herbalist here in La Concha prescribed me a remedy I've never taken before and it seems to be helping.

Flor is using herbs to soothe her girl. Would you like to walk over with me? The shrine Flor has made is beautiful. It's up now on her street corner. They swept the street last night ready for the procession.

She's made stars out of coloured paper her neighbour gave her. I've never seen these before. She's very gifted; such delicate work, and she's finished the twelve dresses and all the wings for the angels.

**Rosa:** Yes, Flor's very skilled with her hands. She has the patience.

**María**: I went to see the girls try on their angel dresses and their mothers couldn't thank Flor enough. The church helped her with the costs. Flor's taking Evita to the church youth club. It's putting on more activities for the children.

**Rosa:** That's good. The children here need somewhere to go. The nuns in my *barrio*, they're doing a lot for the children. Please think about coming to visit, Mum. I'd love to show you the SoyaNica project. You'd like Sister Lupita.

**María:** It's good what you're doing, dear, but I'm too old to be going to Managua. Rosa, there's a bag of beans for you. The harvest this year, you know, was poor.

## Rosa

When I got back from La Concha I went over to see Clara. I was telling her about what had happened in La Concha, about the farming cooperative being attacked. José María Salas, he was one of the biggest landowners around La Concha and now he's back. It isn't right. Most of Marcos's cooperative has gone and so has Lucho's, Ana's man. No one wants to die. The peasants were right about these old landowners.

Clara said there are land disputes happening everywhere, in Nueva Segovia, in Rama. All over the country peasants are selling their land. Since they can't get credit, they've been forced into being farmhands again.

We were just about to have some lunch, when her neighbour Teresa came running in shouting, 'There's a baby down my latrine.'

She was right, we could hear crying. We called on the men next door to help and I ran home to get rope and plastic. When I got back four men were working to lift off the concrete base. I said to a girl standing there, 'Please go heat up some water.' We needed to wash the baby soon as it was brought up.

One of the men lowered himself in on the rope and managed to bring up the baby. Clara said she'd take care of it and we went back to her place, me carrying the water the girl gave me. The baby didn't seem to have anything broken, and when we'd cleaned her she stopped crying. We thought she might be OK.

I left the baby with Clara to go buy a tin of powdered milk and borrow some baby clothes from the centre. When I got there I found a television crew interviewing Sister Lupita. When they heard why I was there they were keen to see the baby, so I took them with me to Clara's.

Clara told them everything that had happened and said she hoped the mother would see her baby on TV and come to her place. That night we watched this on the TV.

Next day people kept turning up with baby food and clothes, but no one came to claim the baby. Leda came over to say she thought we should report this to the police so we asked her to do that. We were expecting a visit from them but no one came. And for the next week no one came to claim the baby either.

Clara said she could go on looking after the baby but by now we were both pretty sure the mother wouldn't show. I really thought the baby needed a medical check-up but Clara worried that if she did, the welfare people would have to be informed and they'd take the baby away. That's why she wouldn't go to her doctor. But a week later, the baby started vomiting up her milk. I said we had to go to a doctor and said we'd go to the one who works for Los Pipitos. He has a small practice, a clinic for babies. He's a good man and I knew wouldn't charge much. It wasn't the first time he'd helped me, so Clara agreed.

He examined the baby and was obviously concerned. He said the baby needed to stay in the clinic, and not to worry, costs would be covered. After three days the baby was still no better. The doctor asked us again what had happened. I told Clara not to worry and tell the truth, so she told him about the latrine. He was reluctant to use antibiotics and said breastfeeding would give the baby a better chance. There were other mothers there with their babies and he asked if anyone was willing to help and one kind

112

woman offered to give her milk. But this made no difference, the poor baby kept bringing up everything.

It's sad to say about what happened. She died after two weeks. Clara was beside herself. She felt guilty but from the start the baby was fighting a losing battle. The post-mortem showed she had a weak heart.

We talked about what we should do and both felt we should look for the mother. We felt she needed to know what had happened; at least we should try. I kept thinking about the girl I'd asked to boil the water. I had this hunch, the way she was watching us that day the baby was brought up.

We went to her house and the girl was in. Marianne is her name. We asked if we might have a word, but she didn't want to talk. I chanced it and said I knew she was the mother. She denied everything, 'You just watch it. It's all lies. I'll report you to the police.'

'Go ahead, do,' I said, 'because they might well ask you some questions too.'

We had to leave it. A week later Clara said a friend of Marianne's had come to tell her Marianne was suicidal. We thought seeing the girl's mother might be a way in.

Clara told Marianne's mum everything and she started crying. 'I didn't know she was pregnant,' she said.

Impossible, I thought. 'You can't be serious. Why didn't you talk to her?'

'No, honest, I never knew. I thought she was putting on weight.'

I thought next she'd say she'd never been pregnant herself. A mother knows. The moment I saw Laura not eating, not sleeping, all tense, I knew.

It was good how we talked this through, and we asked if she'd tell Marianne how sorry we were and that we'd like to help. In some ways I was surprised when she did come to see me. We talked and that's how I put her in touch with Daniel, who's a psychotherapy student, and she's been seeing him. He's doing his internship in the *barrio*. Daniel also takes a class of kids to help them with reading and writing. He's popular with the kids, he has a nice way about him. He's here with two others doing psychotherapy with a group of teenagers, pregnant girls, helping these girls take better care of themselves so hopefully they'll be better able to care for their babies. The therapy is for six months. They do this in the community centre.

We're attracting folk all the time who want to know how we run the kitchen and we're doing training now. A woman, Yolanda, she'd been with us to get hands-on experience making the soya milk and burgers. She runs an orphanage and we took her up on her invitation to visit her in Carazo. A bunch of us Soya women went there on the bus. Yolanda said most of the children do have mothers but they're too poor to keep their babies. The sad thing is they don't find homes for them. That's mainly due to the adoption regulations, they're so tight. When Clara lost the baby she went to see the adoption people but they turned her down. Clara told them her two boys were grown up and away from home and that she was in a steady relationship, but they said the *barrio* wasn't a safe environment. Find me a *barrio* that is. Everywhere is the same with the drugs but at least she's offering a child a loving home.

Did you see Ramón looking over the fence? I've known him since he was tiny. He's taken three plastic buckets from the kitchen and some of Angélica's clothes. I don't know how he does it, in and out in a flash. He steals for his dope, sneaks onto my patio. Poor lad doesn't eat or sleep, just walks the streets. After his mum died he went to bits. Two of us from SoyaNica went with him to hospital but the doctor told us if no one was there to care for him, there was nothing they could do. He comes expecting food and if I give him some and then shut my door, he starts kicking it, wanting more. What to do?

# 5 Kindred spirit

*Eleven years have passed and it is now 2005. Rosa's mother María died in 2001 and Rosa herself was ill in 2002. But her soya project is flourishing. Hurricane Mitch had a devastating impact on Nicaragua in 1998. Veteran Sandinista leader Daniel Ortega scandalized many supporters by signing a pact with the notoriously corrupt Liberal leader Arnoldo Alemán.*

## Rosa

We took food, clothes and medicines on our first visit to Posoltega to see how we could work there. It was Sister Lupita who said I was the person to help. We went in a pick-up loaded down with sleeping mats, mattresses, sheets, clothes, matches, cigarettes. Driving in we passed people digging in the mud for whatever they could find. There was hardly a thing left standing. Posoltega was a sea of mud. People were living under sheets of plastic by the side of the road.

We were told it all happened in minutes, the volcano had sent an avalanche of mud over everything. For days the crater had been slowly filling with rain from Hurricane Mitch until it burst open. The mud rolled down on top of everything. I read that two thousand people died and more than a thousand were missing.

It was horrible, and the saddest was seeing the children. A ten-year-old boy told me he was the only one left in his family. He'd survived three days by climbing a tree, three days!

A man told me he'd come home from Costa Rica to look for his wife and children. He said he couldn't even find where his house had been. His wife and children were gone. Everyone seemed to me disoriented. The enormity of this catastrophe was too hard to grasp. We went to the cemetery and a digger was making a huge communal grave. Bodies had been brought in from everywhere, corpses that had been found many kilometres from town.

The second time we went was to start up a soya kitchen there and I wasn't alone, I went with two other women, a Canadian and a Spaniard. We went to one of the few places still standing: the school. The municipal mayor, Felicitas Zeledón, had arranged for us to use it.

A group of about twenty-five women were waiting for us. I can't properly explain how hard that first meeting was. Some burst into tears. They said they'd felt abandoned. They had nothing to eat but corn. They seemed beaten by misery. Some said before the disaster they'd made a living selling *tortillas*, beans or vegetables. It was heartbreaking. And how could they be so kind towards us after all they'd lost?

From then on I was going there every week. Rigoberta, Leda and Clara and I started making weekly collections around the *barrio* of clothes, cigarettes, salt and things, and every Tuesday and Friday I took the collection to the people in Posoltega. We left Managua at five in the morning and drove a hundred kilometres to get there by seven.

We went for three months to set up their communal soya kitchen. Together with the women, we first built the oven and then over the weeks I showed them all the ways to cook soya. They learned all kinds of recipes. And they worked out how best to run the kitchen to suit the community. We also visited camps for homeless folk nearby to offer to help set up their own soya kitchens.

In some ways it was a similar set-up to the *barrio's* SoyaNica kitchen but their big advantage was that the soya was grown locally so it's cheaper there and that made the whole project more viable. It's so good for you but they'd never used it before. Eating soya like rice and beans was new to them.

I think being there and listening to the women was just as important as the project itself. It seemed to help them come to terms with what had happened, that they had survived and could live again. One woman in the group, Gaby, told me she'd lost her husband and her boy. She took me to the place, a deep gully, and we didn't go further. It was a canyon full of branches. She told me she'd been with her husband when her boy was swept away. She'd told her husband, 'Wait for me, I'm going to find him.' But he'd told her, 'No, don't go, you'll die too.' She wouldn't listen, she went, trying to stay on solid ground, but it was impossible. She had to turn back to where her husband had been. But he was gone. The river had ripped out the ground from where he had been standing. Who knows if he was buried in that mud?

As the weeks went by the women told of everything that had happened. Another woman in the group told me she had lost her sister and a mother told me she had lost all her children, five of them, and her grandparents.

Being there and working together let some of the pain go. The women brought their children every day and together we cooked and ate. We always made enough for everyone. It was great for them to be able to feed their family with just one kilo of soya, and I felt something was lifting. When I got home from a day of working there I was always tired but also felt contented.

When we were nearing the end of the training, Felicitas found a permanent place for the community kitchen right beside the school and those last days were very busy. You see this photo? There I am, taking the class, and here are the children eating soya burgers with soya cheese, delicious, on hot tortillas. And this one was taken on the last day. There are all the women, and that's Gaby. What she

*We always made enough for everyone*

said I'll always remember, 'Here we are, feasting, laughing, and all on soya, and to think how we were.' They'd cooked a feast: soya sausages and soya cheese. And that's the *piñata*, I'd taken a lot of coloured paper because they'd asked me to show them how to make *piñatas*. That was a great day. All the women were there with their children; everyone involved came along, including the mayor. So much had happened over those months.

There was still masses of work going on with the house building; all that was still going on when we left.

I'd love to see how things are now. Hurricane Mitch was seven years ago, 1998. I know the community kitchen has worked out; the women are still making the soya food there.

* * *

Since then I haven't really had any free time to go back. I've been pretty much here ever since, looking after Sara and nearly every day helping out in the soya kitchen here. That was where I

119

got to know Sara's mum, Tania. Tania came to the kitchen to have something to eat. Her family had thrown her out and she was a mess, she was sniffing glue. After she had given birth to Sara we found out she was leaving her baby over at the mechanics' shop because she knew the fella there. He came to tell us. We tried helping, gave Tania powdered milk, but she wasn't in a fit state and she wasn't feeding her.

I thought the Ministry of the Family could help and after I contacted them, they sent a social worker and Tania agreed to talk to her if I was there too. Just the way Tania was made it obvious she wasn't caring for her baby, and when asked what she wanted to happen she looked at me and said she wanted me to take in Sara. That was a big surprise and I was sort of put on the spot, but I wanted to help so I said yes, I'd look after Sara until Tania was ready to take her back. Tania said she did want to clean up and asked if the social worker could fix it for her to go to a drug rehab. So that's what happened. Tania in effect gave me her baby and then went to a centre to try and kick her habit.

From then on, Sara was with us and Angélica really took to her, so much so I had to keep reminding her Sara wasn't ours, that once Tania was better Sara would leave us. But that never happened. We kept hoping Tania would sort herself out but we're talking about years now and Tania is still wandering about out of her mind. She needs her family but they won't have anything to do with her.

Sara has been with me ever since, since she was one year old. It's a pity what happened to Tania. After Sara came to me, Tania moved in with another addict and supposedly he came off drugs and found them some room to rent. But Tania isn't someone who'll ever keep off drugs. She can stop for, say, three months but then goes back on, so some days she'd be cuddling her baby, then the next she'd forgotten the child even existed.

In some ways I reckon she does have her wits about her. She fixed up for all her kids to be cared for. Yes, Tania has five other children; Sara was her sixth and Tania managed to find homes for all of them.

The psychologist from Ministry of the Family told me the most important thing was to give Sara constancy and love. She said Sara would need a lot of guidance and told me what to watch out for as she grew up. The best thing I did for her was to take her with me when I went to the soya kitchen. The women doted on her and that helped her learn quickly to talk, and she's never stopped, the chatterbox, and did she put on weight! She was on a pure diet of soya milk and love.

Angélica and Darío are her godparents. I was very emotional how so many friends came and gave Sara presents at her christening. And when she started nursery SoyaNica paid for her clothes.

At first I was worried her mother's addiction had affected her, or the separation from her or not having her mum's milk; I felt this especially when she started school. She had trouble paying attention and didn't really play with the other kids, but she's OK now, she settled in. I haven't been able to have her properly enrol at the school because she's still not legally my child. I'm still tied up trying to adopt her. The Family Ministry agreed years ago to the adoption but their red tape is impossible, and she's going into fourth year at school.

I hope I've set her a good example. How can I put this: I don't want her expecting something for nothing when I'm not here, so there's no falling out in the family; I want her to continue being treated like she is, like one of the family. My sisters have been really kind, how they've accepted her means a lot to me.

Sara is a lovely girl. She'd love to have a dog and says she'd like to be a vet but I can't see her doing that. She's more suited to hands-on work. She can already handle my sewing machine. And she's a great dancer. I've enrolled her in the folklore dancing class at the community centre.

She's only ten but you'd think to look at her she was fourteen or fifteen. I've been worried about that. At least she knows all about that kind of thing and we've talked about not letting herself be pressured into having sex. I've given Sara leaflets from Ixchen about rape and the games men can play. That's a worry.

*She'd love to have a dog*

Seriously, you visit any maternity ward these days and it's filled with teenage mums. The National Assembly voted in favour of sex education but I doubt teachers spell it out. Sex education needs to be made much clearer.

Angélica, I'm sorry to say, left school when she got pregnant. She was eighteen and she insisted she would keep the baby. She told me she was old enough to make her own decisions, and gave the same answer when I asked how she was going to support the child.

I knew she was banking on my help but I told her otherwise. I was so angry with her and just wasn't willing to pick up the pieces anymore. I felt now she'd done this it was time she took responsibility for her own actions, but of course, afterwards I felt rotten about all the harsh things I said to her. Just before she was due we had a big row and she said she was going to leave and stay with her boyfriend. That wasn't right either. The little I knew about him I didn't like. He was way too young and had no education; he'd left school after primary and just spent his time hanging about, running errands, playing with the kids on the street and I'd heard he took drugs. I didn't know his family and thought best to keep it that way: 'What the eye don't see the heart won't feel'. I only prayed for no bad news. Thank goodness before she walked out I told her, 'Well, if things don't work out, remember you've always your home here.'

For months I heard nothing and I was worried sick. My mum knew Angélica wasn't living at home but I hadn't told her about the baby. I didn't want her upset too, especially because she was unwell. But she could put two and two together and wanted to smooth things between Angélica and me, suggesting I invite Angélica's 'husband' to my home. She wanted to help and I wasn't going to say no to her, but neither could I lie.

\* \* \*

Ah, much too much happened over that period. Six months later Angélica did come home; she came back with her baby. She knew I wanted her home. She wouldn't say what had happened other than they had money problems and that it hadn't been easy. I welcomed her home but I was too busy to pay her much attention, all caught up trying to make money to help pay off Mum's medical bills. I was doing any sewing job I could get and all the family were chipping in also to cover her bills. Her doctor said Mum had a heart condition as well as a kidney problem and that she was malnourished. Flor, Ana, Dora and I all tried to give her rich soups, but she could barely take a spoonful. It was painful trying to coax her.

'Ah, no, I don't feel like it, please, don't bother me.'

'Why, how are you feeling?'

'I've just no appetite for anything. I don't know why.'

We spoke to the doctor again and he suggested to try fresh fruit juice and biscuits but she refused, saying the juice would give her a cold.

I was coming home every Sunday to be with her. We all gave what we could to help her, and were calling Carlos and Sergio all the time to let them know how Mum was.

When she seemed to be getting no better Carlos came to stay. He suggested the doctor prescribe a nutritional milk, but again, she only swallowed the tiniest amount. Her doctor said then to give Mum whatever she asked for and when Dora's husband Alfonso visited and Mum said she'd like some French bread, we thought that was a good sign. Alfonso was gone a good while. He had to go all the way to Masatepe to find the bread but I could see it wasn't the proper sort. Grandma knew how to make that special bread. All the same Mum was so appreciative for his effort and had the bread with coffee. She never stopped liking coffee.

Flor went to call on her church friends to ask them to visit and Mum really brightened up when they came and sang some of her favourite hymns. The next day was her birthday and we asked the church guitarist and the six singers to come, which they did. That was wonderful, seeing her joining in. They really revived her spirit.

That day she had asked for her priest so I went and he said he would come the next day. After he'd seen her he spoke to Flor, Dora, Carlos, Guillermo, Ana and me. He told us, 'When the time comes, it will be as if she's falling asleep.' We knew then all we could do was wait. There was nothing to be done.

That night she became so restless. I asked if her feet bothered her, they were swollen, but she said she had no pain. She just couldn't settle and asked help to sit up, to be taken to the toilet, then to sit again, then to lie down and we all took turns to be with her. None of us slept. The next day it never stopped raining, leaving a chill in the air, so we helped Mum into her warmer nightgown and that night she did sleep much better.

Every day her friends came to visit, to spend a little time with her and when her favourite nephew appeared, you'd have thought everything was back to normal. 'Ah, my dear boy, would you mind fetching the water for Ana?'

'Of course not, don't worry yourself.'

Mum always kept Ana in mind.

That was on the Thursday and it was then she became much weaker. We asked was there anything she wanted and she said, 'Please pray. I want to sleep.'

We were all there apart from Sergio, and mother kept asking for him. Every day we'd been calling him in Costa Rica. He had a terrible time getting home. He needed an official stamp in his passport and because he's illegal there, it all cost him a lot of time and money to get home. Carlos went to meet him off the bus and at four in the afternoon Sergio arrived home and when Mum saw him all she could say was, 'Thank the Lord.' He wanted so much to be able to speak to her, but it was too late. That was how she died, in Sergio's arms. Mum died September 22, 2001.

It was hard on Sergio. He hadn't been with us during those last weeks. The last time he'd seen Mum was on Mother's Day. He broke down. We all did. We'd done everything we could for mother: the doctor, her church friends, the priest, and now she had left us.

We stayed together for nine days. Everything felt unreal to me. Her friends called by and we'd give them coffee and talk but I don't remember much. Everyone brought a gift of food. We had a lot of help from our close friends, offering us plantains, bananas, beans and coffee. But we didn't have enough for the coffin we wanted. That was hard for us. I don't want to talk about this. The coffin was a problem.

I think Mum's faith gave her an inner peace. The way Mum and Dad lived showed that. I know Dad loved and respected her. She was an educated, honest and generous woman.

\* \* \*

At the time I was working at SoyaNica and making a little extra with my sewing jobs, but we were always short now Angélica was home with her little baby, Richie. So when I picked up a big order to make a load of school shirts I was very relieved. This was early in the New Year. I had to dedicate myself full time and when I found I was running out of time I asked Rigoberta, Clara and Leda to lend a hand, but they weren't fast enough so I had to ask Angélica too, but still time was running out.

It was then I had this vivid dream. I dreamt I was climbing a steep path up a mountain and halfway up I heard water rushing and turned to see it rising up fast. I couldn't climb quickly enough and I was terrified I was going to drown. In that moment Dad appeared carrying a huge branch and brought it crashing down into the water and that stopped the water, it changed its course and ran off into a gorge.

What relief to wake up. I thought this dream was about the pressure I was under to meet this deadline. I didn't even have time to eat properly. Leda brought me a dish of cooked meat, enough for both Angélica and me. I thought I must have eaten too fast, because my stomach blew up and I ended up feeling so wretched I had to stop sewing for the rest of the day. I was no better that night. I came down with a fever but next day I made myself keep going on the job, sewing, sewing. Maybe it was my kidneys, maybe the February heat – whatever, something bad was happening. The fever would go down, then it would come back and even worse.

*Dad appeared carrying a huge branch*

On the Saturday, Laura came by on her way to La Concha. She was going there to check on how her new home was coming along. My brothers were doing the building for her. She took one look at me and said I must see a doctor.

'I haven't the time, Laura, this job has to be finished.' But I was no better the following week and did go to see my doctor. He thought I had a kidney problem and told me to drink plenty of water and gave me a prescription for antibiotics. That brought down my temperature a bit but the pain was worse and I just couldn't sew anymore, so I had to ask Angélica to hand in the job unfinished. They took advantage of that; they paid me next to nothing. Had I not been so ill, I'd have challenged them.

As Sister Lupita hadn't seen me for all this time, she came by and when she saw the state I was in went to ask the herbalist who comes to the *barrio* centre to visit me. He gave me a remedy for the pain but said he was unsure what the matter was and said I really needed a medical check-up. His remedy, though, helped me so much I thought I was on the mend and didn't bother with any check-up; it's all money.

But when Laura came by, she insisted I go.

## Laura

I woke up sobbing and Heraldo tried comforting me, asking me what was wrong. I felt icy cold like nothing I'd ever felt before, and it spread through me until I was shivering from head to toe. Heraldo put his arms around me but I was too upset. I got up and went to the kitchen. Heraldo's mum, Rita, was making coffee and I told her my dream, more my nightmare, that I was in my old school with my buddies. I'd gone to find the toilet and when I opened the door I saw standing there a tall man dressed all in black. I felt dead scared and ran back to my friends and asked them who the man was. They looked at me really surprised, saying didn't I know, he was the old school priest who'd died. Ah, though petrified, I found myself going back and I opened the door again and the priest now grabbed my hand and was dragging me in. I pulled and pulled to get away, and that's when I woke up.

Rita said, 'Whatever it means, I'd say go and see how your mum is doing.' She knew Mum hadn't been well with a tummy bug and had a temperature. I agreed with her and took a bus over to Mum's. And a good job I did. She was doubled up in pain. It was lucky too. We got an appointment that same morning with my doctor, Dr Colón. He's very good.

After he'd examined Mum he told us her condition was critical: she had appendicitis. He was amazed she was even able to walk and said we had to go straight to hospital. We were both in tears when we got into the first free taxi and told the driver to take us to the nearest hospital.

We went to Emergency but we were just left waiting. I pleaded with a nurse to help Mum but we were left hanging on. We were there for two and a half hours before a junior doctor spoke to us and when I told him Mum had a ruptured appendix, he said we were in the wrong hospital. Can you imagine! There were no ambulances. Somehow I got Mum out and into a taxi and off we went to the Manolo Morales Hospital, where we should have gone in the first place.

She was in a bad way but she wanted to go by her place to pick up a nightie and wash bag. I begged her to let me do this later but no, no, we had to go home. We drove up and who should be waiting by the door but Dora, Flor and Ana. They'd come as soon as they heard. Heraldo had called Dora earlier on about what was going on.

Seeing them all worried, Mum put on a brave face. She said, 'Oh now it'll be too late to be seen. I'll go to hospital in the morning,' and asked me to make everyone coffee. So while I was doing that I called Heraldo to come over quick, we had a problem. And he did, he came straight away.

It took him to convince her. 'No Señora, you've got to go to hospital, and now!'

All of us crammed into a taxi with Heraldo following on behind on his dad's motorbike to the hospital. By now, you can guess, it was getting late, and we still had to wait.

When a doctor did finally see Mum he said that as critical as her situation was, they needed us to buy all the medicines she'd need, and he wrote down a long list.

They couldn't provide anything. Unbelievable! And we were told that six hours was all Mum had. It was already ten o'clock at night when Heraldo and I set off on the bike. We must have gone to every drug store still open. After an hour we had everything but the surgical thread. We drove to the private Baptist hospital and I begged a nurse there to help, but no, she didn't even look up from the desk.

We had to get back. They must have some thread in the hospital. But the surgeon insisted, 'No, we can't operate without the thread.' Did they really not have any? Mum was going to die for want of this thread. This was the worst experience of my life. Desperate, we drove off to the only pharmacy we'd not gone to in Altamira and yes, yes, they had the thread. Now we joke why we hadn't just gone by Mum's and picked up some sewing thread. But ah, this was a nightmare.

Mum went in for the operation at one in the morning.

*We must have gone to every drug store still open*

We'd been told by the doctor to be prepared for any outcome. Then it hit me: the dream, me desperately pulling back from the priest, pulling back, was trying to pull Mum back from death. We waited and waited, none of us talked. We all felt helpless. There was so little hope. We waited, saying nothing. And Angélica couldn't stop crying. She was like a little girl.

Finally the doctor came. He came and told us Mum had come through. She was alive. Oh, the tears. But he said she was still in a critical condition.

We weren't allowed to see her until the next afternoon. Angélica was first to see her, she had insisted, and when she came back she said Mum was awake and already complaining: 'I've been waiting ages to see you.' I've never been so happy to know Mum was complaining.

Angélica was anxious to be able to stay with her. She could only do that with a special pass, so she set about fixing that. From then on the two of us took turns staying with Mum, Angélica during the day and me in the evenings. I spent all my time looking after Mum. Slowly, day by day, she got stronger and after two weeks she was well enough to come home.

## Rosa

Laura and Angélica took very good care of me, bringing in chicken and vegetable soup, and Darío, bless him, brought me hot meals too. The hospital food is expensive rubbish.

When I was able to leave, my sisters wanted me to go to La Concha but I'd have felt uncomfortable there. Once I was home Guillermo, Dora and Flor kept on coming by, and always with some oranges and bananas. They all took great care of me.

I was told I needed another operation in three months' time. I was dreading it and had no money for the medicines. I turned up for the appointment and was pleased when the receptionist told me to come back in two months' time, but that's why the infection flared up again. Foolishly I hung on till this next appointment and was seen by my same surgeon from before.

'Why didn't you come for the second operation we'd booked?' he asked.

'Because your receptionist said I didn't have an appointment for one.'

The receptionist had made a big mistake. She hadn't checked. Another delay, but as you can see, this wonderful surgeon saved me again.

I really wanted to avoid this second operation because I couldn't afford the medicines. So I was more than grateful to Padre Silvio. He was the hospital chaplain and on every visit he'd ask how I was doing and when he got to know my situation, he must have had words with the staff because they made a collection to help cover my costs. Isn't that kind! He came every Wednesday to see patients and always brought boxes of tomatoes, oranges and bananas.

Now families must come with cash or, like me, hope for some miracle of charity. Now you even sign a paper before they operate to protect the hospital from being sued for malpractice. How different this is from the eighties. When Mum went into the Lenín Fonseca Hospital her treatment was all free thanks to the Sandinista government.

I was allowed home after a week this time. The doctor ordered me to do no cleaning and no cooking for a whole two months so I wasn't going to argue with that. I had both operations in 2002, the second one in September. That was three years ago and now I'm fully recovered. Even going to La Concha last Christmas was fine despite the chill there at nights.

* * *

That first year after the operation Richie was with me most of the time when Angélica was working. I had plenty of time to think. I really needed to come to terms with everything that had happened with Mum, and my illness, and with Angélica. I wanted to be at peace with myself and with Angélica. And looking after Richie helped, yes, and he also helped me get my energy back; I had to, that boy's such a live wire. When he reached one and a half we thought he'd be better off going to nursery. Being at home all the time was holding him back and the nursery is only across the road. He has his routine there – eating, playing – and his talking has come on, he never stops. The nursery has been excellent for him. He knows all the nursery rhymes, remembers

*That boy's such a live wire*

all the stories. The nursery isn't expensive and he gets juice, lunch and a break at three.

At four I pick him up. Angélica is usually home by eight to take over so I can relax then, read or watch some TV. Yes, Richie, he's charged my batteries. He calls me *Mamá*. Angélica is more like a loving Aunty to him. He seems fine when she's away working. He comes to me for cuddles, snuggles up when he wants to nod off, and I'm the one he wants to put him to bed.

That first year Richie was with me, I took to reading the Bible and read again and again those scriptures about forgiveness and acceptance, and found I could be more open with Angélica. Both my girls had been badly shaken by my operations, frightened I was going to die. I don't know if they believed me but I meant it when I told them I'd no intention of dying, 'for the children's sake'. Angélica had Richie before I went into hospital and she needed my help and so does Sara; she has nobody but us. I suppose too I was letting them know they should get on with their lives and stop worrying so much about me. Anyway, Laura isn't in a position to help me much, and Angélica, well she does as she pleases. Saying that, though, doesn't mean I agreed with her joining the Police Force. I didn't want her to join, though it's positive insomuch as it's a proper job.

I can see she's much more confident. The training did that for her. Just listening to her was exhausting; every day she was jumping, running, jogging and learning how to handle a gun. She's trained now in self-defence, which is good. It's too dangerous where she has to go, doing patrol around the *barrios*. She's also done guard duty for a bank, a supermarket and now she's been transferred to a hospital security team. I don't like thinking of the risks she takes. Last week a gang robbed a small lottery collective in the Eastern Market; they were after the prize draw and shot dead the collective's president and a policeman. Angélica told me the police had intercepted the robbery, but the gang opened fire and made a run for it. The weapons they use are a lot more high-tech than what the police have.

Yes, we talk more, and even go out together sometimes. We went with Richie to hear Christmas carols at the Cathedral. Carlos Mejía Godoy was playing and a marimba group, and the Cathedral was packed out. When we were walking back Angélica started talking about Mateo again. He's her new boyfriend. She's pretty childish. She'd brought him home to introduce him. He doesn't live here; he works in Costa Rica in the building trade. 'It's a big site,' he said. 'The job is going to run for a year or two.' Then out of the blue he suggested Angélica could go back with him, together with Richie.

He didn't take a breath. 'I've two sisters there. They'll be happy to help Angélica and we can come back when my job ends.'

135

I was speechless. I wonder sometimes what goes on in that head of hers. And the lad – all I know is he came back to see his Mum. She was very ill and died before Christmas. I reckon he was looking for sympathy in Angélica.

I had to put him straight. 'Richie is only two, and he's a big responsibility I'm not sure you're ready to take on. And look, you've only just met Angélica.' No, I was clear in my mind I'd need to know a lot more about Mateo before letting Richie out of my sight, but all I said to him was, 'It seems jobs in Costa Rica for us Nicaraguans are never secure.'

I hung back until the next morning before speaking to Angélica. 'Are you seriously thinking of leaving? You know you can't go now; you've signed up with the police for three years.'

I don't know. Richie didn't seem to count in her daydreaming about this Mateo. Angélica's wavering is a worry. At times I think Laura was right saying Angélica wasn't the daughter I needed. She's too much of a dreamer.

I was hoping she'd come to her senses now that Mateo has gone back to Costa Rica. I hoped having time in La Concha with the family over Christmas would make her think again. She's so like her dad, always finding excuses to not do what needs to be done. Rubén was always putting off what he said he'd do, like his endless promise to give up drinking: 'Yep, the kids come first,' when they always came last. What a shame. I think her dad leaving when she was so young had a big impact on her. She loved him a lot and his going was a big upset.

* * *

For years we'd not seen Rubén. It was shortly after I'd come home from hospital that Darío told me he was sure he'd seen his dad walk by the house. He said he recognized his wiry grey hair. Rubén had this grey hair, thick and wiry, even when he was young.

I didn't think any more about this until some weeks later Darío told me Rubén's sister had come by to say his dad wanted Darío and Angélica to visit him.

Darío had told her no, that he didn't want to. He still feels hurt by him, and I left that with him. But he must have been thinking it over because he changed his mind. Angélica, though, said she wanted to wait and see what Darío had to say. So Darío went by himself. When he came home he told us Rubén had asked after us. Darío told him about his grandma dying and when he'd said how ill I'd been, Rubén said he'd have helped had he known, but then added, 'Ah, your mum, she wouldn't have accepted my help. You know how proud she is.'

Rubén said he'd joined the Evangelical Church. 'I'm on the path to salvation. I've stopped drinking. Every day I say my prayers with my sister.' And then he invited Darío, there and then, to go with him to his church. What was he thinking of? Of course Darío said, 'Dad, no, you know we're all Catholics.' And then when Rubén started on about the Catholic Church going nowhere, that the miracles were all lies, Darío thought it was best to leave.

We heard nothing more until his sister came to tell us Rubén was in hospital and had asked Darío and Angélica to visit. When they arrived they were told he was in Intensive Care and they weren't allowed in. Sadly, they had to leave without seeing him.

Rubén had ended up there after a whole week binge drinking with his mates during the Fiesta of Santo Domingo. He'd no money for proper hospital treatment. It was poverty that killed him, but his drinking would have stopped him from ever fully recovering. His drinking had completely taken over, until

*His drinking had completely taken over*

this. He was only fifty-four years old when he died, oh, far too young.

Maybe he did pray to Jesus to save him. But I'm sure what he did was go to church for two months and then was drinking for the next two. It's sad, he fooled himself, and no doubt his sister. Forgive me saying this but I think he'd have joined her church to fool her into giving him food and shelter. Poor Rubén, I don't think he held his faith true, here, in his heart.

It was tragic. When we were together it was dreadful watching him becoming more and more self-destructive. I didn't attend his funeral mainly out of respect for his wife. I heard they'd got married in the Evangelical Church. Why cause more upset? I was never married to Rubén. I felt no obligation in that sense and I didn't feel any need myself. Once we'd separated there was no going back. Rubén's father once said to me what a hard childhood our children had, but for all the pain our separation caused the children, I know it was better for them to be without their dad.

\* \* \*

Darío wouldn't be as settled in himself if he had to suffer his dad's drinking. He's grown up such a lot this past year and has the janitor's job at Sara's school. He's been a year there now, tends to their garden and runs errands. He says he likes the job even if the pay's poor. I appreciate what he gives me. Yes, he's considerate, does his own washing, all the things I used to do for him and more. Well, that's until Angélica comes in from work. Then it's, 'Over to you, you do your own washing.' They can squabble, sister and brother. What do you expect? So over Christmas in La Concha, Darío was mostly with his cousins and Angélica with Laura.

Flor, Ana, Angélica and I cooked the Christmas supper at home. It was a real feast: turkey and a pile of *nacatamales,* and for dessert we made our special coconut sweet. We decided on Laura's place to eat, it's more comfortable and only a little way down the road to carry the food. Most of the family came and it was a good evening. I stayed on at Laura's and helped clear up. I don't like sleeping in the old home, not now Mum has gone.

Flor wanted me to stay on to the New Year. She wanted to talk. She's so worried about her girl, Evita, wanting to leave and join her husband in the US. Evita thinks she'll be able to help from there, to send them dollars. Flor asked what I thought, if they should sell their smallholding for the American Dream. I don't see they've any choice. They've medical bills too that need paying. Flor has never sat back but at fifty-two she's no chance of a job. They rely on what their boy Héctor can send them. He left for Costa Rica two years ago. He works in construction.

And I wanted to talk to her about the inheritance. It's troubling all of us. I know Mum had good intentions, wanting the property split four ways, between Guillermo, Marcos, Ana and me. I think Mum hoped if Guillermo inherited the house he'd go on paying the bills and seeing to the repairs. You see with Ana still living there with Lucho and their kids means the repairs never get done. Lucho has never lifted a finger for Mum or Ana or even his own children. Not one of the kids went on beyond primary school. None of her five have any qualifications and none have a decent job. That's why Ana is so hard up.

In truth I don't feel comfortable staying in our old home. And that's sad when Mum had told us all that when she was gone, she wanted us to always feel our home was home. No, I don't like this situation; it's a mess and causing tension.

I think that's why Dora didn't come for Christmas supper, so I went to see her before going back to Managua. And it was on my way over there I bumped into an old school pal, Benigna. We had a bit of a catch-up and I had to tell Dora what she'd done. I thought this might make Dora see how daft she is putting up with Alfonso.

Benigna said she'd finally had it with her man. I hadn't known his other woman lived only a stone's throw from her and she admitted they'd got into a crazy competition. Soon as she was pregnant the other woman had to be too, until Benigna had eight kids and the other woman nine. Benigna said she only woke up to how mad all this was when she added up all the other children she knew her man had around La Concha. She said it came to a grand total of twenty-eight! I had to tell this to Dora, but no, Dora will stay put with Alfonso's drinking and other woman.

Dora wanted to show me a house for sale only a block from her place so we went and had a look. It was really needing a lot of repairs but I could see it could be done and it had me thinking. Both she and Flor have been asking me for ages to come home.

\* \* \*

When I left Dora I took the bus to Managua with Darío and Angélica and then went to see Rigoberta to give her a bag of beans. They'd had a good Christmas, she said, with friends over for supper. But her husband, who used to work as an electrician, isn't well. Rigoberta knows La Concha. Her mother-in-law lives there and I told her about the house for sale and me possibly moving back. But I wish I hadn't. She got really upset. 'You've lived here twenty-five years. I've known you that long.' Rigoberta's one of the founding members of the *barrio*.

She listed all the reasons not to go. 'Flor and Dora are in no position to help you. And every time you go, you come back and tell me the electricity and water had been cut off. And your children, their home is here. Angélica needs you while she's training. And look what a location your house is in, right on the main street. You could easily set up a shop. You know all about plants, making *piñatas* and dresses. Then you'd be in pocket to visit La Concha whenever you liked.'

It's something I'd thought about too, to convert the front of the house into a shop. I could at least ask Guillermo what a conversion would cost. I shouldn't have said anything to Rigoberta about moving. She has enough on her plate. So I just said, 'I know I'd be leaving a lot behind.'

I only started thinking seriously about moving back after Sister Lupita died. She was already quite old when she arrived here twelve years ago. She was sixty, but you'd never have guessed it from the energy she had. She was seventy-two when she died.

141

I was very fond of her. She was a great comfort when Mum died. I could talk to her about anything. The month before she passed away she said, 'Rosa, promise me you'll stay close by our side. You know what's best for the *barrio* and the sisters know you're trusted.' I gave her my word but all that changed after she died.

I'll never understand the nun who took over from her, Sister Prudencia. Within a week of arriving here from Mexico she was making big decisions. She told us our work encouraged poor mothering. How could she say our voluntary work was condescending? How is it patronizing to feed a hungry child? We'd worked years for the SoyaNica project and it had become a brilliant success. But Sister Prudencia insisted we charge the mothers for the soya food and when I asked her why, she said it wasn't viable to give away food, saying the mothers coming were irresponsible. She wouldn't accept that SoyaNica was never meant to be a business. It's for the pregnant women and kids who are in real need. They can't pay. And she also said there were too many women involved in SoyaNica and we'd be better off spending time at home.

No, I could never work with Sister Prudencia. It would have ended in tears. Well, it did anyway when she announced the closure of the project. Yes, it had been subsidized from Mexico, but that's not why the project ended. There are other soya kitchens going strong in other *barrios*. It was down to Sister Prudencia that the SoyaNica project ended, down to one person's attitude. And the way she talked to people, they rejected her. She was left with only three folk working with her, and we'd been forty in total helping SoyaNica. To let that go was dreadful.

Of course we didn't take this lying down. Three of us said we'd keep on working with the other two nuns, Sisters Angelina and Marta. They backed our idea to start up new activities for the Youth Club.

Rigoberta had me thinking about the store idea, and then I thought, instead of a store, how about a mini-SoyaNica, scaled down and done from my home? It might just work. If I extended the roof out over the patio to cover a few tables then folk could come and eat there. Some of the Soya women might join in; we could pool resources. If we sold our soya milk for less than cow's milk, folk would come and that could subsidize the mums who couldn't pay. It'd certainly make more sense than dressmaking. The market is swamped with cheap, imported second-hand clothes. What I'm thinking is that Rigoberta and I could set this up together. Why not? Look what we've managed to do over the years: SoyaNica, the natural medicines, literacy classes, the workshops and the Youth Club.

* * *

No, I'm not down even if there's plenty reason to be. Evictions are going on everywhere and public services are being cut to the bone. I mean here too, in the *barrio*. You remember all that trouble we had to save Angélica's school in 1994? Well, now eleven years on, and the threat of closure has come back to haunt us. Back then it was the landowner wanting to demolish the school. Now it is the Ministry of Education's turn to have a try. The parents had to campaign anew and this time it was Sara with her school mates going door to door with a petition. Everyone in the *barrio* signed and the kids went with their parents to hand this in to the Ministry of Education.

At our next Parents' Meeting at the school someone from the ministry came and we were surprised and delighted when he said there'd been a change of heart, that the school was to be renovated instead.

Was this sounding a little too good to be true? We thought so and asked the teacher, Doña Hernández, if she could check this

143

out and sure enough, she came back and told us the ministry was indeed planning to do a makeover, but in order to privatize the school. Like us, she was furious. 'It can't be privatized! No one has the money for higher fees.' So we kept on banging on the ministry's door until finally they did back down. But maybe we only won because the plan wasn't financially feasible.

Anyway that gave us the thumbs-up to renovate the school ourselves. The Parents' Council raised some money around the *barrio* and extra donations came in from Helping Hands and the Lions Club. With that money all the rotten floorboards and toilets were renewed, and there was enough for every pupil to have a desk and chair too. All those years Angélica went to school she had to take her own chair. She carried it there and back. She

*She had to take her own chair to school*

had a bald patch to prove it. It's a great thing to still hear the kids playing in the playground. The parents pay a small fee and for the first year the pupils are given a free glass of milk. When we won this I came off the Parents' Council but I keep abreast of what's going on.

It's one thing after another. Now we're expecting a hike on electricity. Clara hopes the *barrio* will protest but even my SoyaNica pals are too tied up nowadays trying to make ends meet, baking *tortillas* and sweets to sell. Probably they're thinking they can't stop this happening anyway. Most folk here have lost faith in the politicians. No one I know wants Daniel Ortega leading the Sandinista Party anymore. No one I know supports him, not after him making his pact with Alemán. The two are drunk on power and corruption. Alemán got away with robbing the country blind. The court gave him an amnesty to go on living like a fat prince on his farm.

Our new archbishop, Leopoldo Brenes, was on a TV talk show. It's a good show put on by Carlos Fernando Chamorro. What the archbishop told Carlos Fernando was right. Carlos Fernando asked him if the Church was influenced by any political persuasion and he said, 'No, we're here solely to serve the people, as any politician should too. If people don't vote in the coming elections the fault will rest entirely with them. Whoever is next elected president must answer the needs of the hungry and poor. If not, the people may have to find their own solutions.'

Now that was strong, but I don't see it happening. Leopoldo Brenes was telling how he'd been on a visit to farms not far from Managua. They grow pineapple and *pitahaya* for export and he'd gone to hear what the peasants had to say. They'd told him they could get no credit to sow the beans and maize, and Brenes was asking why we're exporting to the US but not growing food we need to feed ourselves. 'We might not be able to change the world, but we can grow enough for us to eat.'

It's the big agro companies exporting the best of our pineapples and meat. That's what CAFTA, the US – Central America Free Trade Agreement, was set up to do. I switch off the moment I hear talk about this 'Dawning of a New Era'. We've been waiting years for this supposed new era. I'm clear this CAFTA era is only to take out our raw materials for cheap. This was why Sandino fought in the 1920s, to hold onto our resources: the rivers, forests and mountains. They belong to us. CAFTA was set up to finally cement over our independence.

Do you know about the deals these companies have in the Free Trade Zone? Those assembly plant owners pay less for electricity and water than we do in the *barrios*. Marcos's girl, Demaris, has a job in the Free Trade Zone near San Marcos. She's in the same sweatshop where Ana's girl, Indiana works. It exports clothes to the US, importing the raw materials to send the clothes back made up. She's a cutter, earns about twenty dollars a week for a ten-and-a-half-hour day. She's in constant debt.

# 6 With my family

*It is 2008. Rosa is now fifty-six and decides that it is time to move back permanently to La Concha. Daniel Ortega is President again, following the elections in 2006 that brought the Sandinistas back to power. But the party is divided and many are critical of Ortega.*

## Rosa

I went to see Dora María Téllez when she was on her hunger strike. She chose the Metrocentro traffic circle because it's one of the most public places in Managua and everyone driving by saw her.

Hundreds of people went to visit her there. I talked to a couple of farmers who'd come all the way from Río San Juan. They were coming to show their support: 'Life's got to get better. There's got to be a way out of this.' It sounded like we were back in 1978. Comandante Dora María spoke to everyone. She's much respected; she has a big reputation from way back to her days fighting against Somoza.

She had gone on her hunger strike to claim her political party's right to political representation. She was left with no other option. She was making a stand, a stand for the ideals Sandino fought for, and there are many others like her who have left the FSLN.

When I got to talk to her I told her I'm a Sandinista and always will be, and how that means I can't support President Ortega; I can't be a Danielista. He's shifted way too far from what the revolution stood for. Power and ambition have taken him somewhere that's beyond any moral principle. What a betrayal to embrace Alemán, a politician who has stolen more money than even Somoza did.

When Daniel Ortega won the 2006 elections I had at least hoped we'd see programmes start up to tackle everything that's fallen apart in the *barrios*. I'm still waiting and I'm not fooled by this Communal Development Credit. It isn't anything other than a scheme to whip up support for him and his wife.

She's the real power behind the throne. Daniel Ortega is never seen in public without First Lady Rosario Murillo. She's like the government spokesperson, in fact like the Head of State. You'd think we were her subjects the way she talks.

María Téllez was protesting against all this abuse of power and the decision by the Supreme Electoral Council to annul the legal status of her political party, the MRS. It was acting on behalf of Daniel and his wife when it did this. We'll see what happens when the demonstrations start. If it's anything like the protests in León, the police will be under orders to attack the protesters.

Daniel won with only thirty-eight per cent of the vote. If he'd needed fifty per cent he wouldn't be President. He only got there through his pact with Alemán.

I've discussed this with my brother Carlos. He was home for Mum's memorial we held in Flor's home. He doesn't want to hear any of this. I suppose it's different for him living in Matiguás. He's told us he's going to stand for the FSLN in November's municipal elections. He's well known for what he's done. He's been living there twenty years and he's been working on the government's 'Zero Hunger' programme, saying how it's giving many small farmers access to credit.

To qualify for this you have to already have a hectare of land, so this programme can't help the poorest of folk. I asked Carlos what President Daniel means with his slogan, 'Rise up, rise up, you wretched of the Earth'. The only way I got a loan was through the *barrio's* Women's Fund. We set it up way back and I had to put up my sewing machine, the house and my bed as collateral. If I hadn't got that loan, I'd be still paying off some loan shark.

I think Daniel Ortega's FSLN has turned into just another self-serving party. Even so, I can see where Carlos is coming from. He's deeply committed, from way back when he went to teach on the Literacy Crusade and for all he went through fighting the Contra. He's suffered for the revolution, and since settling in Matiguás he's dedicated his life to improving the farming cooperatives. It's because of folk like him that the social programmes kept going there despite it all. He says illiteracy has increased, but apparently not to the same extent it has in my *barrio*.

He's always coming up with some bright idea, getting on with his next project. He no longer teaches in the school but wherever he goes he's called Prof. Carlos. He took up agricultural engineering and knows all about soils, cattle rearing and the environment. Carlos made a huge effort to qualify in this. And he's set on his children doing the same, going on to higher education. He's happy there and so is Blanca; she has a secretarial job and knows how to use a computer.

He'll be here tomorrow to buy a motorbike. Flor's son-in-law Paco is selling it to him. He imports vehicles from the States so Carlos will get a good deal. He has too far to travel to go by horse. He has to cover the whole area around Matiguás.

Yes, his world is totally different from life in the *barrio*. Anyone who can afford it has put up a high fence around their place. The *barrio* is now a no-go area, a Red Zone. Any truck driver making a delivery risks having to pay protection to the gangs or be robbed, and that goes for the shop owners too.

The big gangs in the *barrio* are the Puntarenas and Montoya families and they are fighting each other all the time. One week a Puntarenas is killed, the next a Montoya; it's never-ending. There have been children as young as eight dying. And the number of kids now on drugs, lads who I knew were good and honest, are now dealing. A hundred, two hundred dollars a day is a fast track out of poverty. These gangs have got a hold of the *barrio* and a crack now runs right through its heart. Everyone is cautious and wary.

I kept a hand in with the Youth Club for the sake of the kids. The club gives them an alternative to drugs. The church funds it. The smaller kids come because it's a safe space. It's theirs to relax, be themselves, clown around. Some are in a theatre group, some in karate classes. We have good links with the university so students still come to do sports with the kids and teach reading and writing. It's a positive thing for the kids to be with these youngsters from outside the *barrio* who are doing something with their lives. These students are pretty much running the youth groups; they take the kids on outings to show them there's another world out there.

Only very few folk knew our priest was actually meeting regularly with the police to try and tackle the drug problem. In the club we had contact with some dealers through their mums. The drug problem is out of hand. The only way to tackle this is to think big with a kind of Literacy Crusade but about drugs. What I mean is it'd have to be targeted. First I'd do a national census to find out why there are kids every-where selling chewing gum or washing car windows at the traffic lights, and then find their parents, the mother in the market selling ice and *tortillas*, and have real jobs on offer. And then get the kids back into schools and nurseries. To do this is down to having vision and commitment, rather than big resources. It would come down to giving support to each individual.

Take Ramón, the lad who stole my buckets, who grew up with my Darío. Remember I told you how after his mum died he started taking drugs. I'd see him wandering the streets, he was sleeping rough. Well, I went with him again to see a doctor but the medication he put Ramón on made him a bundle of nerves. He needed these pills but he had to take them with food or he'd get really agitated. I said to him, 'Ramón, what's up? What's going on? You were never like this.'

'It's the pills, they're killing me,' he said. We talked and I agreed to feed him and asked Rigoberta to help too. But we couldn't be there for him all the time, so I suggested to him, 'Let's see if you can stop these pills. I'm going to try and cure you with my plants.' I boiled up leaves off my lemon tree with aloe vera and other herbs and left them soaking overnight, and every day for two months he came to take my remedy, and as God is my witness, he recovered. He was as good as new in mind, body and soul. Seeing him recover was no less than seeing a miracle. He'd been unbalanced for years and no one believed anything could be done, including myself.

His sisters had banned him from visiting. I thought, well, now they'd want the good news and went over to ask them to take him back but they weren't interested. 'No, no, he'll not stay like that, he'll lose it again.'

'Really, he has changed, he's better. Just see him once and you'll know. All he needs is food, you'll see.' And that's what happened: they took him in. I went a couple of months later to see him and he was doing fine. He'd managed to get a job at a garage. He'd gotten better within two months and at next to no cost. The plants all came from my patio.

I never had money enough to do anything about the Soya Kitchen idea. And if I had, I'd have been trapped at home, never able to leave for fear of a break-in. The venture was too risky. Whenever we went out we worried we'd come back to find the place robbed. I was worried to go out, day or night. My neighbour was shot in the foot, but she refused to report it; she was too scared her kids would then be next.

In ten years' time cocaine will be like buying a Coke. Managua's a time-bomb. How was Richie going to stay out of trouble? I worried about Darío too, that he'd be mugged. Well, Angélica being in the Police Force, that's another worry altogether. All this had me thinking about La Concha again. I'd think maybe I was fantasizing. I questioned, what did I have really in common with my brothers and sisters? We'd led such different lives. And would the children adapt to living there? And finding work in La Concha would be hard too.

Every morning I woke up with all this going round and round in my mind, and feeling kind of empty. For all the friends I had, life in the *barrio* had changed beyond recognition. In La Concha I had Flor, Dora, Ana and Laura, and it was down to them and their care that I'm alive today. And I knew if I was living in La Concha, I'd be more support to them.

Every morning I'd wake thinking about this, weighing up the pros and cons: the children, the *barrio*, my purse, the family, until at last it all fell into place and I was clear. I said, 'Yes, moving to La Concha is the right thing to do.' It was only then did I talk this through with Angélica, Darío and Sara, and they all agreed the move would be good.

Leaving was the hardest decision I've ever made. I had roots in La Concha but in the *barrio* I had so many friends, so many good folk I'd worked with in the *barrio* committee and community centre. Twenty-five years is a long time. When we started we were only five in the *barrio* committee, then we grew and grew to ten, then twenty, and we did whatever was needed from water taps to land titles. What achievements: the school, the kids centre, and SoyaNica.

Of course La Concha would not be the same, but I knew too it would not be that different and I'd be the same Rosa, and what I did in the *barrio* I could do in La Concha.

One by one I started telling my friends in the *barrio* we were leaving and everyone asked me not to and to think again. They wanted me to stay. The women's group asked if I'd come back for the Saturday meetings but that wasn't realistic. I said I'd first have to sort out where I was going to live and that would take time.

\* \* \*

It took three months before I found a place. Every time Flor or Dora found anything affordable they called, and my lucky star

*I had roots in La Concha but in the* barrio *I had so many friends*

appeared when they told me about this house. It all went unbelievably smoothly. I managed to sell my place in the *barrio* for quite a good price. And then the day came for the move. I went to say my goodbyes to Clara and Leda, and to Rigoberta. And we said of course we'd be seeing each other again.

Guillermo had come with a truck he'd hired and we loaded on the beds, cupboard, cooker, table and the sewing machine, and then we all got on as well and off we went to La Concha.

The new house was nearly habitable, so we could move in right away. My brothers are building another room for the boys and Darío at the back. I've enough left from the sale of our place in Managua to have them install a shower as well. They're good to me, my brothers, keeping the costs as low as they can.

The children seem to be settling in fine, though Darío needs something to occupy his time. He says he'll try for a job in the Free Trade Zone in San Marcos. He'd be OK on quality-checking the T-shirts. He'll be able to do that. I must remember, if he gets an interview he'll need references, police certificate and his work card. I can see he's more relaxed being here with the family around, and Sara. You know she dropped out of school last year. She wasn't making any effort and yet dreams of being a vet. She'll have to be satisfied looking after the hens. She's more suited to doing something like dressmaking or hairdressing. She'd be out partying all the time if she had her way. I've had to rein her in. 'If you want to make something of yourself, you're going to have to study.'

She's very like Angélica was at her age. I suppose that's a good point, because look how Angélica has stuck at her studies. Sara's still young, maybe she'll become more motivated when a little older. In two years Angélica will be qualified and then be on a better wage. She says she needs this training at the university to graduate. I understand from Dora's husband it takes six years of study to become a police superintendent. I don't know what he earns, but it's definitely more than when he started in the force.

Angélica says it's been the right decision to move here, and I know it is. It was terrible – her boyfriend beating her up. When she told me she wanted to keep Mateo's baby, I had to help. I couldn't turn my back on her this time. I knew his violence would only get worse so she accepted my condition that I'd help only if she stayed away from Mateo. And she knows this has to be a two-way street now. We're a lot more relaxed with each other. She needs me to care for her boys, and they're much safer here. I even let them play out in the street with their pals from school. Growing up here will be much better for them.

That's all I ask: to see them grow up into fine, healthy men. Yes, so far, touch wood, I'm fine. I'll be fifty-seven this year. I still want and need to work, and I've had some ideas. Dora is keen too. We've been talking about working together with Flor selling baby clothes. That's one thing where no one buys second-hand. No one gives a new-born second-hand clothes as a gift, and we know there's no competition here in La Concha. Women have to go to Jinotepe, so a baby shop here would save them the bus fare. Dora could make the clothes and cot covers and Flor wants to make *piñatas*, and my place isn't far from the town centre, which makes it a good location. We could sell cosmetics and perfume, eau de Cologne. The front will need to be made very secure.

We decided against selling foodstuffs. Beans and rice don't last, and you know what happens: we'd be dipping in when we went short. Products that keep; that's capital, that's what we need to sell. Last year I had a pile of school shirts left over, all big sizes. I've stored them at Laura's and they'll be good to sell before this school year begins. And I haven't forgotten my herbal remedies. I gave my medicinal plants to Rigoberta. I'm hoping to grow herbs at Dora's. They grow well here in La Concha, the climate's perfect.

I'm glad to be nearer to the family. And there's time to talk. You've spoken to Laura. How happy do you think she is? She had a really good job before she married. Laura's smart and before she met Heraldo she used to be ambitious, wanted to become a business personal assistant. She didn't have to throw that in but she did. But it was Laura who wanted to live in La Concha, not Heraldo. He only agreed to move if their older boy stayed at school in Managua. She says she's happy, but I don't know.

## Angélica

Everyone said I was crazy to join the Police Force. 'That's a man's job. Go and train to be a secretary or a nurse, anything, but not the Police Force.'

It was a big decision to make but I wasn't crazy. I knew that as soon as I signed up. The training has made me much fitter. We were exercising every day and part of the training was in the mountains. We were walking for days and that was incredibly tough going. We were wet all the time and hungry. On other exercises we had to cut our way through undergrowth and crawl through swamps. We had to climb down the outside of a three-storey building, scary stuff, and there was no backing out.

We've been trained to be able to respond to any situation, even a hurricane or military situations like an invasion. I've become a lot more disciplined, I had to be to learn by heart all the Nicaraguan laws. For six months I didn't stop. It was pure stress, especially going on patrols. How old was I when I joined? I was twenty-five.

When I graduated in 2006 I was given a post with the Huembes Hospital Internal Security. I cover anything from official functions to taking receipt of weapons. I check in all the admissions from the Military, the Police, Fire Brigade and Immigration, and also any prisoner coming in for treatment.

Hundreds of people pass through the gates. A lot are workers from the Free Trade Zones. Some companies have taken health coverage with the hospital.

Mainly I'm operating the gate for ambulances and directing patients where to go. Sometimes my shifts can run over and can be as long as twenty-four hours, and then I get the next day off. I'm happy enough. There aren't many posts with free meals. That's the bonus. We're one of the worst paid professions, especially when you think about the risks we take. I'd just started the job when a doctor was mugged right by the gates, in full daylight. A lad grabbed her bag and I went running after him firing into the air and he shot back. Then I aimed and missed just as a biker passed and picked up the lad and off they went, the lad shooting back at me. It was close. I dived behind a car.

It's not so much 'you live and learn', it's 'if you live, you learn'. It was only a week after that near-death experience I opened the gate for an ambulance and on the stretcher was my friend, Julio, a policeman. We'd trained together.

He and his mate had chased a guy who'd stolen a taxi. They followed him out of Managua to Ciudad Sandino. The road into Ciudad Sandino is a dead end so they reckoned the driver would turn back. They set up a road block at the town's entrance and sure enough, the taxi came back. They pulled the driver over and when Julio asked for his licence, the driver shot Julio and the other policeman. Julio died on the way to the hospital. The other policeman is alive.

Julio was only nineteen. Just like me, he'd qualified only ten days before. He died for lack of experience. That's what killed him. How do you break this news to a family? His partner took it very hard. Thank goodness they'd had no children, but they weren't married so she hasn't any compensation; that was given to his mother. After his funeral our police chief awarded Julio with a Posthumous Honour for Bravery but his mum said to me, 'What's the use in an honour? That won't bring him back.'

That's why I've taken out police life insurance and have an incapacity policy to cover me and the family. I wonder if I signed up or signed *over* my life. Thirty years is a long time to survive in the Police Force. Gangs deliberately recruit young kids because they can literally get away with murder because the Adolescent Code protects them.

I've attended a number of short courses with other police officers from El Salvador, Guatemala, Honduras and Mexico and talking to them, I see where we're heading. They can't believe we still patrol unarmed and sometimes not even in units. They say we must be mad or brave or both. The police from these other countries patrol in armed units. I'm only armed at the hospital but I don't take the gun home. Yes, we are brave. The gangs are using explosives, submachine guns, grenades. We're not as bad as Mexico, but not far behind. The police are the enemy now. Folk have no respect or fear like they had of the National Guard. In Somoza's times, when the National Guard ordered you to stop, you stopped. Now we're more likely to be knifed.

Those police officers who infiltrate the gangs too often pay the ultimate price. They play the role and can't back out when the gangs are fighting. Captain Pérez was killed in a gun battle with a rival gang. That's what scares me and everyone else in the force: dying in the line of duty. Sure, there have been times I've wanted to run away. Richie has said to me, 'Mum, when I grow up I'm going to be a policeman.' What can I say? I pray he changes his mind; he's only a little fella.

The course I'm on now, we're learning about the mind-set of delinquents to be able to distinguish among them and know how and when to act or when a situation can be contained without violence. It's a hard call. How to stop these minors without harming them? How do you judge? In my initial police training I was on patrol in my *barrio*, where we used to live in Managua. We caught four men dealing drugs and the next thing the locals had us surrounded and they were yelling and pelting us with whatever, and this went on until the squad pick-up came to our rescue.

We took them in but it didn't end there. The mother of one of those four lads started harassing me. Every time I was home, she'd come asking for a word, trying to squeeze me, asking what I was going to say in court.

She said, 'We've known each other since you were a kid. You used to play with my boy at school.'

'Ah, Señora, it's one thing to know a face, another to know what's going on behind it.' Then she tried to buy me so I told her, 'For your sake I don't think I heard that. You should know my job's worth much more to me than your money.' But another person might have given in. You know, those two paths: the one the police should take and the other where the police get in with the dealers, or in on a robbery, or have an addiction themselves. Sure, if they're exposed, they face the Military Court and that's tough. It's not the Civil Court, and those caught outside the law face a heavy sentence.

Another time I was on patrol with four other police officers in my *barrio*, one of them said to check out a small girl. She was just standing about, not playing or with anyone. She was no older than Richie. I went over and asked her, 'Sweetheart, are you lost?'

'No, I'm waiting for Mummy,' she said, pointing to a woman. So I went over and asked the woman. 'No,' she said. 'She's not mine.' So I go back to the girl, 'Well, who's your Mum again?' and she pointed to another, 'Her, over there.'

'Now no more lies. I'll take you to your real mother when you tell me where you live.'

'No, I'm waiting here for her. She's shopping.'

I was the only woman in our patrol so I was the one to search her. She had thirty-two bags of crack on her, a girl of no more than six years old. Kids doing drug-running is nothing unusual, or a mum hiding drugs in her baby's diapers.

We caught an eleven-year-old boy, and that hit the press. A white Toyota taxi was seen picking up this boy every day from District Four. We tracked down the driver and he said no, the kid wasn't his; he was hired to take the boy on a round trip with some stop-offs. Obviously his way out was to cooperate and that made intercepting the kid easy, and seeing where he was going on his daily deliveries of crack.

The boy was far more scared of his gang than of us. Soon as he knew he'd only have to see the Family Ministry he told us everything. When we spoke to his mother she played dumb: she'd thought her boy went to school and had no idea about the taxi or what he was up to. We put her and the boy on a Restriction Order and she knew if he got caught again, she'd take the rap. But I know if a parent hasn't set their kid right by the age of ten or twelve, there'll be trouble ahead.

Before, in the eighties, that boy would have been sent to the Correction Centre for Minors. Instead we have to depend on the Family Ministry, and it's not functioning. You see the staff sitting around behind desks, turning a blind eye to all that's going on for these street kids. We've too, too many at risk. The ministry is far too slow for what we need when it comes to finding sufficient evidence to hand to the Attorney's Office, so the criminal walks free.

What's the point of me making the arrest if we're not given adequate time to prosecute? When I arrest a delinquent I've only forty-eight hours to bring his case before the prosecuting attorney. That's no way enough time to find witnesses and gather in all the information to compile the evidence. And say the victim or witness can't come within the allotted time, then the case is dropped. That's the pressure we're under, a two-day deadline. Yes, we need to be professional, but that's far too little time.

* * *

Thirty years in the force isn't realistic but for now I have to stick at it, at least until the boys finish their schooling. What other option is there? Every day more and more kids are on the streets selling, collecting rubbish, cleaning cars just to feed themselves. They can't afford to go to school. It's not just the police living on the edge in Nicaragua today; everyone is. The move to La Concha has been for the best, especially for the boys. I'm a whole lot calmer knowing they're fine. If they're OK, then I'm OK.

Mum takes care of them when I'm away. I think she likes being there for them because she had to be away working when I was small. She was never home. She was gone when I woke and I was fast asleep when she came home. And it wasn't much different when we moved to Managua. I'd come back from primary school to an empty home and I fed myself. Plenty of times there was no food in the house so I'd go by myself to buy milk and biscuits.

It was very hard when Mum and Dad separated. I missed him so much; he loved me. I didn't see Dad again until I was fourteen.

Mum couldn't give me the attention. Often she couldn't make the parent meetings. I did my best but in secondary school I wasn't making the grades and I had to repeat a couple of years. At eighteen I left to try and do a computer programming course but in truth the only thing on my mind was my boyfriend Mickey. He worked in the Free Trade Zone and I got pregnant to him. He was really pleased and said he wanted us to live together. We went and rented a room, but maybe that wasn't the best move because I found out he had another girlfriend. I was so upset and told him to choose. Obviously you see, he didn't choose right. After six months I was back home with Richie. We had money problems as well. Mum and I, we had our differences over this. And I know I've made a few mistakes. But tell me what family doesn't have their problems.

Not long ago Mickey showed up here in La Concha. He came, he said, because he wanted to see his son. He said he wanted to help. But I thought, why now and why raise Richie's hopes? Maybe it was pride on my part but I didn't want Mickey thinking I needed him so I said no thanks.

Why allow him back into our lives after all these years? Richie doesn't miss him. Yes, maybe back then, when I came home to Mum's and had nothing then. That was tough.

I picked up a job in the Eastern Market and was working as hard as Mum had ever done. I was out the door by six in the morning and not home till seven, and when I had to go to the wholesalers I wouldn't be back till nine. A year and a half of that shop assistant job was enough. That's when I thought of the Police Force: regular pay, promotion, a real job.

I know at that time I wasn't in a good place and that was when I met Mateo. It was only after I married him that I put two and two together, about how he got his money. I didn't want to see the guy for who he was. I wasn't thinking straight. It wasn't easy; I was pregnant again with his boy, Iván. And marriage is a serious commitment. It was hard but he wasn't treating me right and I was risking everything. His drug dealing would have ruined my future.

I don't have a boyfriend now. My focus is getting through the police course and once I pass this second part of my police degree, I'll be on better pay. Without this degree, promotion would take an age – thirteen years or more to be promoted. Basic police training is just that, basic. Now I'm looking to four years and then I'll be on better pay, and I'll have the chance to do the work I want to, investigating murders and accidents.

This is my first year on the course and my only expenses are food and travel. I'm taking advantage of what's on offer. There are some who can afford to do this degree without working but that actually leaves them at a disadvantage when they qualify because they'll have had no real life experience. It's very demanding, this working and studying, but so far I've managed not to miss a single class. I make it fit. If my security job clashes with the morning class, my workmate at the hospital covers for me.

## Laura

I felt Mum was lonely in Managua. Living near me and her sisters makes life easier. Yes, she's much better in every way since the move. I'm doing her accounts, keeping on top of the costs for the building materials and what she's paying my brothers to improve the place she's bought. She trusts me. She tells me what's on her mind.

I don't think she can rely on Angélica that way. Angélica isn't considerate enough. I thought she'd have grown up a bit after all Mum's been through; that she'd be more appreciative of what Mum does for her. She never seems to think about anyone but herself. Of course I don't say anything. She'd only fly off the handle like she did when I said her kids weren't Mum's responsibility.

'Mum doesn't mind caring for Sara. Why should she mind caring for mine?' That's what bugs her. She feels Mum loves Sara more than her.

OK, I know I shouldn't wind her up but I can't help it. 'Now you watch tubby Sara doesn't grab your supper.'

Angélica is right though, Mum's way too soft on Sara. She'll tell Angélica off, 'Now don't you be ordering Sara about, telling her what to do,' when it's Sara who's ruling the roost. Sara is a lazybones and doesn't take a blind bit of notice what anyone says. She should show more respect, she's a lot younger than Angélica.

Maybe I'm a bit harsh but that's how I see things. I can't really tell though. I'm looking in from the outside, and perhaps that's the same for Mum, in the way she sees us two. Mum doesn't really know Heraldo. She's never liked him and I know she thinks he was a bad choice.

She doesn't give credit where credit's due. We only have our home thanks to him; well, and to me, and God. And the boys, he's always there for them, happy to pay for whatever we need. Allan has asked me to ask his dad for a computer. It'd make sense; the town's internet cafe is expensive. We could then down-load anything we wanted. The cheapest I think is around four hundred dollars. Used ones cost less but have less memory too. No, Heraldo has never said, 'There's no money.' He works so hard he's hardly here during the week. He never takes a proper break. He gets home late and has to be off first thing in the morning.

Most of my free time I'm alone with my youngest boy, Gabriel. He's at the local primary. My family and the job keep me busy.

For two years I've been on the Credit Cooperative committee and there's always something new to learn. I'm gearing up right now for the co-op's forty-third anniversary. The president, the vice president, treasurer, secretary and representative member will all be coming. I have to present my report to the associate members. Others will be reporting on their areas too, like commerce, housing and farming.

It's a big co-op; it provides services for three thousand associates, so there's a great deal to manage, all done by several committees each made up of three people. They manage security, credit, welfare, commerce and education. The Security Committee ensures the whole business operates properly and that's the committee that's on top of me.

I pray my post is renewed. If the associates want me back they'll vote me in. I'm pretty well known. We'll see what the outcome is this Sunday.

I like seeing the money put to good use. Before any loan is approved I have to check if they'll be able to repay and that's important because the money belongs to everyone. My job is to evaluate how secure their guarantees are. The co-op can receive up to thirty requests a week so I'm kept busy. I'm so much faster than when I started in banking, mainly for having a computer. I still take the initial interview down by hand.

Each request we check through how many loans the associate has had and their repayment record. If they have a steady income it's easy getting a loan. It's harder for first-time borrowers, they need references. The interest isn't as high as the bank but defaulting is costly. I've enjoyed learning all this. The loans are mainly for house building, commerce and wholesale produce. We can provide start-up loans, say, for a shoe workshop or a beauty salon. Growing up here has been an advantage with the job.

La Concha has always been home to me even when I was living in Managua. I grew up with Granny. Myrna and I went everywhere with her. Granny was my first teacher; I loved her classes, loved how she taught. She taught me how to read and write. She gave me my start in primary school and that kept me ahead all the way up through secondary school.

And when I left to go to technical college in Managua I was always home at the weekends. I was keen to keep studying but not to leave La Concha. Mum was keen I get training and have a career, so that's why I moved to Managua and went to night school. I stayed with Mum and studied accounting, and worked during the day. Myrna came too and we went to college together. My first real job came through my internship in BANIC, working in its Credit Assessment department. I must have been good because they offered me a job. That was when I was typing by hand with a typewriter. I was phoning our branches in Jinotega, Boaco and Matagalpa to total up their costs for the bank manager to see outgoings against expenditure.

I regret not renewing my contract. After the three years were up I took redundancy. I thought if I change my mind I'll find another banking job easy enough. Rosa tried to persuade me to stay on the job but my heart was beating for someone else. I'd met Heraldo and all I had on my mind was love and marriage. It was only after we'd tied the knot that I added up our expenditures but there were no banking jobs going. I ended up working as a secretary for an engineer Mum knows. It was OK but after two years I was going nowhere so became a sales assistant because the bonus pay was good. Rushing between their three shops wasn't, though, and when sales were poor not only was there no bonus, but the boss went nuts, yelling at me like I should force customers off the street to buy the shoes.

So I applied for a job with a small credit union, the sort you see everywhere. They offered me the post of promoter and the pay was good with travel expenses included. It meant visiting their different associate groups. I'd manage about three a day and usually I was done by three. It was easy and the year flew by.

Then the coordinator asked me to deliver some cash in Acahualinca, the *barrio* near the lake, when the associate was home. This was after sundown and the *barrio* had no street lighting. It was pitch black, and nobody was out but the dogs. I was terrified I'd be mugged; the place is worse than Mum's *barrio*. I was shaking like a leaf when I handed over the money and the gentleman saw I was in no fit state so kindly walked me to the main road and waited until I got the bus. I felt lucky to be alive. Then the coordinator asked me to move onto debt collecting – and you know how hard it is to pay back once you've spent the money. This day we'd gone to collect off a market vendor and we waited and waited until the coordinator asked if I'd hang on as he had another collection to make. Hah, when eventually the vendor showed all I got was a mouthful of pure filth. You'd have thought I'd come to steal off her. It was the same having to ask folk for a guarantee, like a television or fridge, as if I was robbing them. No, this was not the job I'd applied for. Even if it left us short I had to quit. That was in 1997.

The trouble was Heraldo wasn't earning much. It was my mother-in-law, Rita, who came up with the idea to sell hot food in the evenings. I'd be safe at the front of the house. Next morning she lent me the money to buy meat, plantains, rice and beans in the market. By evening I had everything ready for folk to buy, folk on their way home and too tired to cook. I soon had a routine going and for the next few months kept this food stall going, making a fair amount. I did that until I met Linda at

Mum's. She was there in the barrio translating for a foreign delegation visiting the SoyaNic project, the one mum helped run. We got chatting and I liked the way she was dead open and direct. She kept looking at my hands and asked how come they were so stained. I told her from cutting plantains and told her about my food stall. Then she said, 'Well, I don't know if you're interested but I'm looking for someone to mind my boy. Would you consider working for me?' I was surprised but I suppose Mum was my walking reference, and there and then I accepted her offer.

Six months later Heraldo found a better-paying job with a white goods outfit and said he really wanted me home looking after Allan. I didn't want to leave Linda but I didn't want to argue with Heraldo either. I felt sad to go, but she understood.

I'd only been home a month when I got this call from a familiar voice: 'Laura, you remember me? Linda's friend Pierre?' Pierre was a French documentary film maker and he and his wife, Pastora, a very nice woman, had stayed with Linda. He said, 'We're here in Managua and we'd love it if you'd come work for us.' Pierre was offering good dollars and that persuaded Heraldo.

I stayed with them nearly three years, right up to when they left the country. I was ready to stop anyway. I was five months' pregnant with Gabriel. Yes, I gave birth to him in 2001.

We'd been living off Heraldo's wages and saving all of mine. I was putting the dollars to one side for us to move to La Concha. I had saved enough to buy the land after my first year with Pierre and Pastora. I'd always wanted this and when a plot near Granny's came up for sale, I went for it. The next year I saved up enough for the building materials and the next year I asked my uncles to start building. I was coming and going until we had enough to pay for the roof and could move.

All the time they were working, Granny would come down the road to bring them coffee or fruit juice, can you imagine. She was really looking forward to having me nearby. When I first moved to Managua she was always waiting for me to come home at the weekends, waiting with a little present. 'Here, I've made this for you.'

I loved her and so wanted to be near her. She was very close to me and Myrna too; there was no difference. She treated everyone with such affection. I wanted to care for her like she had for me. I called her Mummy. Ever since we were small, Myrna and I had always been with Granny. 'Let's go to church', 'Let's get ready for the procession.' We were never left behind. We went with her everywhere, visiting friends, going to collect this or that donation for the Virgin of Carmen. 'I'm here for the Virgin of Carmen Fiesta', and we were always made welcome.

After I married there was no one accompanying her to church on Sundays and I knew she felt alone. She was always asking, 'When will you next be home?' 'You'll come, won't you?'

I was going to look after her. I wanted her to move in with us so I could take care of her but this wasn't to be. She wasn't here to see us move in. The house was still unfinished when she died. We only moved in 2003 when the roof was put on.

Towards the end Granny couldn't go out much and she was left alone a lot of the time. Aunty Flor would visit but she has her own cares. Granny tried to visit Flor, to walk on her own, taking the short cut through the back. She'd been gone hours and Ana wondered where she'd got to, so sent the children looking and they found her. She'd stumbled and had been lying there on the ground all that time. Why hadn't someone gone with her? She should never have been alone. When I came home at weekends we'd go together to see her grandchildren. We'd walk over to Flor and to Dora. She wanted us all nearby.

In truth, I felt Ana was offhand with Granny. Myrna told me how Granny had gone to stay with her for a couple of days, walked all the way to her place. She said Granny had said she wanted to be with her. That showed how alone she felt. Myrna had felt something wasn't right and she was right to think so.

We have to keep going.

It took till last December before we had the house complete with the floor laid with white tiles. That was Heraldo's 'bright' idea. Mum thinks I was daft to accept. My uncles and cousins did a fine job.

I feel lonely at times, especially with Allan away at school in Managua. He's going to a good school there but I do miss him. Some days I take the bus to Managua just to see him. I know he'll be back on the Saturday, but five and a half days is a long wait. I have Gabriel of course. He's just seven and as smart as his brother. He's top of his class and a little tear-away.

I've told both boys, 'I want you two to study like it's your best friend, like you're going out together. Then you'll discover what a fantastic world this is.' Allan is way ahead in fifth grade. I'm certain he'll sail through his exams. He wants to go to university. He has a bright future ahead of him. Yes, I'm very proud of Allan. He has extra tuition on Saturdays to improve his English.

You see lots of kids skiving off, even middle-class kids, even rich kids attending private schools. I've seen them in the middle of the day hanging out, smoking. Maybe their parents aren't there for them. It's incredible the way these kids can behave. I blame TV, the soap operas. Indiana, she thinks the same as me. She went to work in the Free Trade Zone to make sure her children get an education. We're both making sure our children get on.

It's a shame the amount of poorer children too who aren't at school. Their parents can't pay for the books, uniforms and shoes. Hunger and unemployment are everywhere. It's tough. Anyone in a proper job is because of some personal contact, and permanent contracts don't exist. If you haven't seen someone for a while, just ask and for sure the answer will be, 'Costa Rica'.

I pray my boys get on and will fulfil their dreams. It's for their education their daddy works so hard. I joke with Heraldo he'd be better off staying in Managua. Then he'd have no time left to waste on drinking. At least he's stopped on Sundays.

I heard him talking to Carlos about fighting the Contra. He said he hardly drank before then, that it wasn't until he was discharged that he started drinking. I think he experienced too much horror and became disillusioned with life. Carlos doesn't seem to have this problem; he keeps his drinking under control. He's too busy to waste time. Carlos was here buying a motorbike.

I've learned to take things as they come. It's the only way; stay chilled, for the children's sake and Heraldo's. And tell me honestly, what marriage doesn't have its problems?

Every New Year it's the same resolution. 'New Year's Day I'm stopping', and he'll stop for a month or two, and say how much better he feels. But you can bet on our next outing to go swimming in Laguna de Apoyo he'll open a bottle of beer and there he'll be, back boozing. He knows he's pouring money down the sink. Maybe if he joined the Evangelical Church he'd fix his problem. A guy I know was telling me how that church saved him. I couldn't join though. I'll always be Catholic and I'll keep praying to God to wake him up and show him how he could be. I wonder if he inherits this drinking from his granddad, who died from sclerosis of the liver. Heraldo's brother, Oscar, too, was in hospital; he couldn't move for intravenous drips. He had no escape when Heraldo, of all people, spelt out his options. The doctor told him the same, but Oscar wasn't listening. The boys were very upset. Allan kept asking their dad if Oscar was dying. It was me who told Allan, 'See your uncle, he was heading to be a big baseball star, like you're going to be.' His uncle was a fantastic pitcher, had a super strong arm. Now he's in his rocking chair all day long.

Heraldo tries kidding himself that the boys don't see, but of course they do. He knows what he's doing but he's got something in him. I've begged him, 'What will it take, your mother dying?' I said that because he knows that's what it took to stop Marcos and Guillermo, it took them making an oath on Granny's deathbed. I pray that he quits before I get too bored to bother anymore. I have the house. He can go if it comes to it.

## Marcos

I've wanted to build onto my existing house but the materials are unaffordable. The government promised jobs but it's hard to find any construction work. Building materials are too expensive and the pay is minimal for what work there is. This unemployment allows people to take advantage, forcing you to accept whatever's on offer. The poor fall into that trap. Everyone says we're worse off than before. Two of Flor's children have had to emigrate. They've taken their chances, but not all of us can; the journey costs a lot. I'd say the life we live is precarious. My two girls, one works as a cleaner and the other in the Free Trade Zone. She's a qualified accountant but hasn't found any auditing work. We made a big effort to find her work. Maybe the new mayor will help. He's a friend of mine. I'll put this to him after the coming elections, he might help her. One of her children is at the local school, in the preschool class, and her other is in fifth grade; and my other daughter's child is in fourth year.

Because father was a farmer and mother a housewife we couldn't achieve much. At least I stayed in school two years into my secondary education. Since then, from fourteen years onwards, I've worked in construction, first with an uncle, my mother's brother.

In 1978 I collaborated with the FSLN. I wasn't a fighter but I helped, right up to the present, supporting the party. There was hope for change at a national level back then. We Nicaraguans, we were looking forward to a better future. After 1979 and the Sandinista victory, the agrarian reform helped and farming cooperatives were set up here. I left my cooperative: it was poorly run and I didn't agree how the founding members considered they should have more say than members like me. This didn't sit well so I resigned. In the end they sold the lands to someone with money in Managua. Now lands are ending up in private hands again and that's a step backwards.

We had hopes this present Sandinista government would bring improvements, but corruption in Nicaragua is like it always was. For all the effort we poor make, there's no progress. I think this lack of progress is also because of matters beyond our control, and making things too expensive. Some blame the government, others the president. But whoever's at fault, one thing is for sure: in the eighties we could afford to eat; now, even beans and rice cost too much.

So we stay here. If any one of us has a problem we try and help out, but that's not possible for those who've moved far away. That's reality. I thought of going to Costa Rica myself but realized I'd be spending all my time working just to feed myself and feeling bored, having to do everything myself, wash my clothes, make my food, every day the same old thing, and living in rented accommodation.

## Dora

Pilar will mend a trouser or blouse if it pays well. I thought she'd pick up dressmaking from me but she hasn't the patience. The only other work is in the Free Trade Zone. A friend of Pilar's said I might get a training job there. She said she'd talk to her supervisor but I told her no. I felt embarrassed. I'm too old. Only women between eighteen and thirty are taken on.

I'm working right now for a charity. They're in Masaya and run courses on sewing and beauty and how to use computers. I teach a crash course in dressmaking and I'm paid well enough for the hours I do. It's mainly mothers who attend, wanting to make clothes for their children. Last week a delegation came from Korea and the tutors gave them a presentation; it was quite formal. I showed them what I taught and while it's self-evident, I explained that if we had more space for industrial sewing machines, the women could be trained up to be ready for work in the Free Trade Zone. We're cramped and short on even the basics like chalk and rulers.

Sewing to sell in the market makes no business sense. The last dress I made at home was beautiful. The woman gave me a photo from a magazine to copy. I made up the pattern from that and had it ready in time for when she said. And I waited all day for the woman to show. In the end I was chasing her, the shame of it.

'You didn't come for the dress.'

'Ah, yes. I'll come by tomorrow.'

And when she did, she only paid half of what she owed. Those who pay on time are the well-to-do, but where are they? I thought making up sheets would be a safe bet, be sure to sell, but I haven't even paid off that loan. Every time I pass the money lender I look the other way. I know everyone is in the same boat, but it's embarrassing.

*The last dress I made at home was beautiful*

I worry how I'm going to feed the grandchildren. I worry about the cooking gas. I worry about having to barter for beans and rice, because bartering with my neighbour is awkward. We've had no gas so William, my son-in-law, cut down the old avocado tree but the wood smokes and takes longer to cook.

The tree stopped producing fruit; it was tired, like me. The tree used to produce hundreds of avocados. It must be over eighty years old. The one in our front garden back home, where Ana lives, still produces. Dad planted it and he told us all to plant a tree 'so your children's children will never go hungry'. And he was right, we've lots of sweet and bitter oranges, and coconuts from planting years ago.

Where the avocado tree stood was the place to grow plantain, but Alfonso planted the plantain where I've squash growing and now they're blocking out the sun so the squash can't grow well. He does things like this.

I can't rely on him. I never know when he'll show up. He never says, 'I'll be over on such and such a day.' It took him a year to fix the latrine and all he had to do was move it to the other side of the house. It's easy for him to say, 'Don't worry, everything's gonna be alright.'

When I first married, yes, I was happy. It was his other woman I couldn't handle, and he was spending more and more time with her until he'd as good as moved in with her. It still upsets me that he's with her and their two kids. It took eight years before we actually separated. I got by on the money I'd saved from the sale of the sewing cooperative. I'd set up the co-op here in La Concha with some pals and we did well for the first couple of years. This was soon after the Sandinista revolution. It was the war against the Contra that reduced sales. That war left not just us poor, everyone was left short. We'd no choice but to sell up. We all felt very sad that day, dividing up the money among the nine of us and going our separate ways.

Pilar took it very badly when Alfonso moved out permanently. She was so upset I took her to the doctor and he said her problem was anxiety and depression.

I had to call Alfonso. I told him, 'Pilar needs you. If you don't come and your daughter dies, it'll be your fault.' For two weeks she was in hospital and Alfonso did come. Pilar was only seven years old at the time. Now she's twenty-three.

It was never easy between Alfonso and me. After he said, 'I come here only to see the children', I made sure to be gone when he came and with the children. When we came back in the evening his mother would say, 'Where've you all been? Alfonso was waiting here all day.' It was no business of hers where we were. She's why Alfonso is like he is. He doesn't know what love is.

I do my best. For four years I took Mauricio to Managua on the Sunday and brought him home on the Friday until I got him into another special school nearer to here. I went with him there until he was sure about going on the bus alone.

He left the school when he was fifteen. His teacher said he was getting into trouble with a rough bunch of boys. How was I supposed to teach him? I arranged then for him to go to Los Pipitos in Jinotepe to learn carpentry, tailoring and pottery but he refused to go. He wouldn't tell me why. It's a pity; he can't take in much. He's not been right, ever since he caught meningitis as a baby.

His brain has been affected. I couldn't step outside the door without him crying and he wouldn't speak. Now he's grown up he's more sociable. He went with Alfonso to see the horse parade go through town; it was the Fiesta of San Antonio. Alfonso took Mauricio for a nice day out only to end up frightening the boy. Alfonso said a drunk lad started calling him a Sandinista B and wanted a fight. At least that sobered Alfonso up; he's not drinking and not losing his temper so much.

That was when Alfonso asked me to take him back, but I told him, 'Not if you're still with her. I can't have her standing between us.' I can never relax. No, I'm here for my children and only for them. The place doesn't belong to me; the house and grounds are his. I'm here until he throws me out and I'm sure he won't do that as long as his children live here. He cares for Pilar: on her fifteenth birthday he offered to pay for her to go to technical college. I was keen for her to go. I was planning my week to take her there, to Granada. She could have come home at the weekends.

177

But instead, she'd been keeping secret she was seeing a lad. When I found out I told her what I thought and Alfonso too told her she was far too young.

It was because we didn't approve that she ran away. We were at our wit's end. I told Alfonso he was to blame. I didn't know who her boyfriend was or where to find him. After two days and fearing the worst, the mother of Pilar's boyfriend came to tell me where she was. Pilar was staying with them and she'd begged them not to tell me. It was the father who told her I had to know. Oh, what a relief, but it was a shock when the mother told me their lad, William, wanted to marry Pilar. She said he was training to be a mechanic and she seemed to be really fond of Pilar. She said they were happy for the two to live with them.

No, I wasn't happy about this and I didn't think it would last but it has. William is a good guy and we get on fine. They've moved in with me now. His mum often drops by, always with something for the children. They have three now. After they had their first two boys, William said he wanted to try for a girl. I told them this 'trying' was mad and, now they've their third boy, William agrees with me.

He's sensible enough and can turn his hand to whatever needs doing. What's the saying, 'A home is empty without a man'? He's the handyman at the Catholic University, does the carpentry, painting, gardening. One of the nuns hired him to do a private job for her and afterwards she came all the way here to visit us. She said how he's valued at the university. She must think highly of him.

Pilar needs to find work. We've talked about her running a food stand at the front here. But then Alfonso said I'd just put on weight, the cheek. He's right though, saying we'd not be able to compete against the store selling subsidized basic grains. This is government trying to control prices of basic foodstuffs.

It's popular with folk. A lady I know in Las Sabinas was telling me how they're all for Daniel's government. 'We've been given hens, a sow, a cow with calf and goats.' They've a smallholding so that's how they qualified for the Zero Hunger programme. They feel gratitude; that's why they'll vote for Daniel. But is that any different from when I was made to vote for Somoza? When I was young I worked like Rosa, for a big family. The family had connections to the Somoza family. I saw Somoza's son visit the house. The family made sure all their servants – the gardeners, maids, everyone working for them – voted for Somoza and I did what I was told. I was young and innocent. I voted with the rest of the servants. That's how Somoza won. They used us. That's how it was, that's what they did. Our votes were collected up and taken from the house. The elections were fixed. The method might be different now but isn't the end the same?

## Carlos

I joined the Sandinista literacy campaign just after the revolution, in 1980. I was seventeen and wanted to be part of this Crusade. I was sent far away, to El Almendro, Río San Juan. The campaign recruited thousands of students like me to teach people to read and write. Back then over half the population couldn't read or write. We volunteers shared our bread of knowledge and also helped the families with their farming. I pulled my weight doing whatever was needed on their land as well as teaching. I knew farming but many students were finding out for the first time the real cost of having a plateful of beans with a *tortilla*.

The experience had a big influence on me and I made my mind up to become a proper teacher. And so I did; I studied to be a teacher and on my internship was sent to Santo Domingo in the department of Chontales. Teaching the children there was the start of a long career. After I qualified I was moved to Ciudad Sandino, a new town outside Managua, to teach children there for a year.

I then applied to the Ministry of Education in Managua to work on the Adult Education Programme, making improvements to the original Literacy Crusade methodology. And there I met my lovely Blanca.

I struck lucky in love. Blanca and I moved into rental accommodation in Managua, and we married. We managed OK until our first son was born, then we had to find a bigger place. We first thought Masaya would be good because it's close to my family in La Concha, but we couldn't find work there so, with no home and no land and with our little boy, we decided to move to Matiguás because Blanca's mum and dad lived there. I knew this would mean leaving my own family behind in La Concha, but it worked out for the best.

We resigned our posts and moved. Matiguás is a beautiful part of the country. It was a major change for me. Luckily both Blanca and I picked up teaching jobs straight away, and we joined a housing cooperative and I soon felt at home.

All our spare time was taken up building the co-op's new homes. At the start we were living with Blanca's parents and every time a house was finished we had our fingers crossed we'd be the winners of the raffle. That was how the co-op handed over the house. But it took till the birth of our third child, Mónica, before we were the winners. I think that's why I was voted president of the co-op, for the amount of time we gave before we had our own home.

At school I wasn't just teaching primary children. I ran classes for the older ones, and set up a project for the kids to grow corn and beans and rear rabbits in the school grounds. This was their little fundraiser. They ran it themselves to have a fund to pay for their pencils and paper.

Blanca and I worked so hard but our wages barely covered our basic needs. We'd come this far and with three kids to think of, we realized we had to find better paid work. That meant both of us going back to college part time while still teaching. We had to do it.

The college was some way from Matiguás and one week we were so short of money Blanca had to walk there and back; we didn't even have the bus fare. But all the time we were telling each other, 'You can do it', until we actually did. Blanca qualified in business administration and I in ecological agricultural engineering. Now, a whole eighteen years later, I can tell you how correct that decision was. At the time, though, folk would say things like, 'Look at you two, going all that way and what for?' I'd just tell them, you're never too old to learn. And in the end some actually followed our example. They made that effort to study in Matagalpa, went to college themselves and now have a worthwhile job here in the community.

Blanca was the secondary school secretary here up until the Sandinista government came back into power in 2006. Since then she's been the Adult Education Study Circles promotor in and around Matagalpa. She's out all the time going wherever a class can be set up.

All three previous governments let this work slip and illiteracy crept back up to twenty-five per cent here in this region. It's even higher in other parts of the country. There's now a push for everyone of all ages to learn again from primary to secondary levels. Most youngsters realize they must at least have that level of education.

Blanca coordinates the teachers' programmes to fit the students. She sees how to set up the classes for farm workers and the aim is that in six months' time, illiteracy will again be something of the past.

She loves her job, and me too. Working in agricultural engineering has allowed me to be part of so many worthwhile projects. Right now I'm setting up agricultural training programmes and I have another job with a cooperative, an organic coffee collective. I'm evaluating its output and looking at how the members can invest their profit to improve their community the way they want to. Basically I'm helping them plan to build what they want from their collective capital. The cooperative is affiliated to UNAG, the National Union of Farmers and Ranchers. Ah, and I didn't say: it's a women's cooperative. The women had been selling their coffee only within this region. Now they're improving the coffee processing with new machines, so soon they'll be ready to export. The way they work together in their cooperative has pulled them out of poverty. That's why they invested in the machinery. It's win–win so the government gives them backing.

I'm also helping the local producers' association improve the bean production. It's a good feeling seeing these projects grow. I think many appreciate what we've done, Blanca and I. They saw us arrive, saw us teach and then work to improve the farming here. For some time I'd been thinking of running on the ticket with the present mayor in these 2008 municipal elections. She's a Liberal and, like me, sees our alliance as an asset. She thinks we'll be more able to deliver what we promise by working together.

The former governments of Chamorro, Alemán and Bolaños never delivered. For twenty years folk have waited patiently for a light to go on. When I visit the communities the problems come tumbling out: homeless families, hungry children, the elderly. 'We were promised electricity, homes, road repairs, water, employment and credit.' They won't stop saying, 'We've heard it all before', until their troubles are fixed. We've never promised what we can't deliver and I know they know that. That's why I think we'll win this November.

The top priority is to have maintenance done on the local schools, which are falling apart, and to make the credit system more easily available to small farmers. And then, new nurseries are needed for single mums, like on the coffee cooperative where I work. The sceptics are the old Liberals, and they'll always be with us, but no one can deny how the Rural Credit Fund is helping small businesses. I know plenty of women are clubbing together to take advantage of this, setting up to sell *tortillas*, sweets, cakes, that kind of thing. The Venezuelan government is behind this and that's how the new nurseries will be funded.

Most folk you'll find in Matiguás are Liberals, just like their parents and grandparents were, and few have ever set foot outside Matiguás. They want nothing to do with the Sandinistas. It's not like Estelí, where so many died fighting the Somoza dictatorship. The people there have a deep understanding of why they are Sandinista.

All the same, I've seen how folk in this region have slowly shifted in outlook over the years. Once Liberals and Sandinistas were poles apart and that has caused a lot of bloodshed. But over these twenty years they've seen who's sorting out their problems and who isn't. To date sixty-eight peasant families here have received the government's basic farming products package called Zero Hunger. Each one is worth one thousand five hundred dollars and includes a cow, a sow, hens, and also fencing, cement and zinc roofing to build a shed for the animals. The farmers also receive seeds so they're feeling real changes. And with the reintroduction of the ENABAS stores, no one needs to go hungry with their prices.

Why would anyone vote against this new credit funding? This fund I'm involved with is a revolving fund geared to helping the small farmers plant their beans, maize, rice and plantains. The low interest rate ensures they have a good return, which they only pay back after they've sold their harvest. This keeps the fund expanding for other farmers to access. Folk know this wasn't available under the previous governments. It was want of credit that forced far too many to leave their land fallow and, worse, to sell. The funding is slowly turning this around. A lot of land is being brought back and a good bean harvest can sort out many a problem.

That's why so many farmers are attending the agricultural courses we run. We're teaching how to conserve water and stop soil erosion and now many small farmers are reintroducing plants to prevent this erosion. The plants also benefit the soil, putting back nutrition.

Everyone can see if we don't do this, don't reintroduce these plants now, the land will be arid within five years. It's a serious problem.

Another solution to this is the new clay eco-stove. It uses far less wood to cook with than an open fire so both money and trees are saved. And farmers are being encouraged to plant fast-growing trees around their holdings to coppice. That way they go on growing and help slow down this erosion.

My UNAG friend Miguel and I were invited last year by the Guatemalan farm co-op union to go there and tell them about all this union work. But honestly, it was us doing the learning. What unbelievable odds they're up against! With no support, their indigenous women leaders have set up their own credit system and run a very impressive agro-ecological cooperative. Their co-op also has a social fund to help their members in all kinds of ways, right down to funeral costs.

Their way of working, their co-op values, made me think of my parents because they held the same values of respect and being responsible and being giving. I'm very grateful to Mum for showing me how precious these values are. Her love of learning turned every book I read into a discovery adventure. I've a lot to thank my parents for, and what they gave to see I had an education. And now Blanca and I are doing the same for our children. We're doing everything to see our children go further.

For all that, I know there aren't the jobs, even when you've gained a skill. There's a whole young generation unemployed out there. And why goes straight back to the last governments we've had, from 1990 onwards.

And not only in our country: throughout Latin America you can see governments have handed their economies over to the free market. You can't compete in a free economy when the playing field isn't level. How can a small peasant farmer here compete with mega agro-industry?

## Flor

Paco buys trucks and buses in the United States to sell here in Nicaragua. He takes part payment on delivery, say two thousand dollars for a bus, and the rest paid in instalments. He's finding business slowing down. He's back down now to collect.

It's some years since he left for the States. Before he left he said to me, 'You know when I married your daughter, it was to be with her, to live with her.' He always wanted Evita to join him.

'Yes, that's only right,' I said. 'She should be with you.' Paco is a responsible man. He loves her, loves her like he loves his girl and always intended that she would join him. So this year she made the decision and we all helped.

Before she went she told me, 'Mum, if it works out for me, then it will also work out for you and papa.' She said she even wants to buy back our land. We had to sell the holding to pay the medical bills. And what was left went towards Evita's journey.

The US Embassy turned down her application for a visa so the only way was overland. She left home at eleven o'clock at night on May 13 this year, 2008. Paco came for her and they went together with their girl Janette, his sister Daniela's two children and our cousin Francis. They had to catch the morning coach to Guatemala, which leaves Managua at two in the morning.

They reached Guatemala with no problem and picked up another coach for Mexico. They reached the border in three days but there they had trouble. Border Police boarded the coach. They had talked about this, about everything that might go wrong.

The police looked at Evita's documents and those for the children and they were let through but Paco couldn't risk being searched. He didn't trust that the Border Police wouldn't keep his passport. It would have been the end if they'd taken it because it's precious; it has his US visa. He kept it hidden so he was taken off along with other undocumented travellers.

Evita couldn't say anything, she just had to sit tight and watch him being taken, and they were left to carry on alone. She hadn't ever been away from home, this was her first time travelling far, with so much responsibility for the kids, poor girl.

She knew they had to get off the bus thirty kilometres inside Mexico. Before she left she'd studied the map and knew the route like the back of her hand. Every day she'd been looking at the map to memorize every road all the way to the US. They got off at

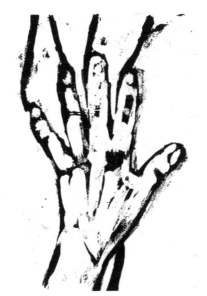

*She knew the route like the back of her hand*

a garage and she called someone Paco knows, a Señor Gómez, and he came and picked them up and took them to his place.

She called us that evening. She was in tears and told us Paco had been taken off the bus, and she didn't know more. We were all very worried for her, for the kids and Paco. Rosa, Dora, Guillermo, Ana, friends kept coming over, asking for news, 'How are they? Where are they? What's happened to Paco?'

Then two days later Paco appeared.

He told us he'd been in a Mexican police cell with eight others and the next day put on a bus back across the border. After paying the police a bribe he barely had enough to come home.

He'd called Evita so she knew he'd be back as soon as he could raise more money. We gave what we could; we had to ask friends and we gave him five hundred dollars and his mother gave the other five hundred, and with that he was off.

This is the first I've seen of him since he left so it's only now I've heard the full story of what happened. He told me getting back into Mexico went without a hitch and he found Evita and the kids waiting at Pedro Gómez's house. Pedro had arranged for a *coyote* to take them north but he charged more money than Paco had. Paco had to call his sister Daniela in the States to ask her to wire him the money. When it came through, they started their journey north with this *coyote*. They reached a big city, Guadalupe, and Paco took them to stay with another friend of his.

Daniela had a contact there Paco needed to find. Two years before, this man had arranged for Daniela's crossing into the US and it's a dangerous crossing. Paco wanted to see this *coyote* boss because he handled the route all the way to Houston. He said the guy demanded a lot of money. Mexico is a lawless country and the border's a death trap. Paco paid for his family to cross the Río Grande in an inflatable dinghy. He needed to be sure they'd be as safe as possible, but nothing's certain. He said too many folk are caught walking across the desert. This boss wanted more than Paco had and in the end they struck a deal to hand over the final payment when Evita and the children arrived in Houston.

Paco then had to go on separately. He was crossing legally on his visa, driving in. He had to leave Evita and the kids to go on their own. He told Evita he'd be waiting for them on the other side. Evita left with Janette, Francis and Daniela's two. They went with only water and a few clothes. They left in one of two trucks with around seventy others – men, women and children – and they travelled until nightfall. When they stopped and got down,

*They were rowed across the Río Grande in an inflatable dinghy*

Evita and the children were separated off from the other travellers. She doesn't know what happened to them.

They were taken by two *coyotes* to the river and after inflating a dinghy, they were rowed across. Paco said it was supposedly a crossing under less surveillance, a wide part of the river. It took time to reach the other side.

One *coyote* took them through undergrowth. Evita was carrying the smallest and they had to be quiet. When they reached the road another two men were waiting, one with a car and the other drove a truck. Daniela had arranged for her children to go with the driver of the car. He had his wife with him and they were going to make out they were a family.

The truck driver told Evita, Janette and Francis to get into a concealed compartment above his sleeping cabin. It was tiny. They squashed in and the driver told them to lie still but they

189

couldn't have done anything else. They knew they had to because the border control has high-tech surveillance that covers kilometres on either side of the border. That's why they had to stay still.

Paco had told Evita what to expect at the border. He'd told her, 'The truck should stop for no more than twenty minutes. If any longer then be prepared because the Border Guards will be checking the truck.'

When they came to a stop Evita was in agony. Her shoulders and spine had been rubbing against the roof and Janette and Francis were very frightened but she told them to be quiet.

They heard the truck driver say he was transporting tomatoes. Then they heard a gringo tell the driver to pull over. Then they could hear sounds coming from the back of the truck.

Evita prayed, 'Dear God, I beg you to save us.' She thought this was it, that the truck was being fully searched.

Then she heard, 'OK. Drive on.' The engine started and slowly they moved off.

Evita could then tell Janette, 'Don't worry. Soon you'll see Daddy.' Paco had told them he'd be waiting six kilometres on and that the driver knew where he'd be. But when the truck stopped she heard the driver say, 'They're not coming down until Houston. She'll call you on arrival. That's the boss's orders.'

Paco called to them. Evita was too scared. She just said they were all OK.

They drove on and on, and all the time Evita's shoulder was bleeding from where it rubbed against the roof. They were squashed, thirsty, poor things. It sounded more than terrible.

Many hours later the truck stopped and at last the driver let them out. They were that stiff they could barely move.

They were in a big parking lot. The driver told them they were outside Houston and gave them water. He then gave Evita a number to call and Paco answered. Paco told her, 'Don't move from there. Someone's coming for you in a pick-up.' He told her to ask the pick-up driver for that same phone number and not to go with them unless they got it right. Evita was terrified but she stayed calm for the children's sake, and they waited. Hours went by, and all the time the truck driver was keeping an eye on them.

A pick-up finally pulled up and a man got out, a Mexican. He told Evita the right number and took her, Janette and Francis to Paco, who was waiting for them at his sister's. Their nightmare was over.

Paco told Evita the boss in Guadalupe had called him when he'd crossed into the States. The boss had raised his price and told him to pay his associates in Houston. That's why they hadn't been allowed out en route and why they'd waited so long in the parking lot. Between robberies, bribes and the final ransom, their journey to the US had cost thirty-five thousand dollars.

Paco said he's going to need time to pay this off, years. He'll be off again soon, flying back.

Paco's doing his best; he's already repaid what he owed us. And Evita, she has a heart of gold. She sent us all little presents, imagine, for her Aunty Rosa, for Angélica, for everyone, toys for the children and blouses and T-shirts. She must be saving every dollar she can. She's had a cleaning job for three months now. God is looking after her. Evita only gets off work on midday Saturday and is back working on the Monday.

Daniela has a residency permit so is secure. It's different for Evita; she's undocumented but I don't see her coming back. She's gone for good. In time she might even see some of that beautiful country. She'll settle in. She called to say they were all fine when the hurricane hit Houston. They'd had no electricity or water for a couple of days but their flat was OK.

We have to look forward. Who knows, maybe one day I'll be able to visit them in the States.

* * *

If it wasn't for Evita and Héctor, we wouldn't manage. Héctor left for Costa Rica when he was twenty. He's still single. It's his sense of duty towards us that's stopping him having his own family but that's not right, not having a girlfriend after all these years. He's said he misses home but there's no work here. Soon after Evita left, my husband Enrique said he wanted Héctor to come home to help him with his carpentry but I told him we'd manage. We're indebted to Héctor; he's a good son.

We can't go on like this, depending on them. Dora and I, we've talked about setting up a small business. We could pool our skills if Rosa came on board. Rosa has an idea to sell baby clothes, and Dora, she could make some of them, and my *piñatas* and decorations would sell for birthdays and engagements, and I can do flower arranging for funerals. All it'd take is everyone in the family to invest what they can. I only need scissors, glue, dyes, string, wire and card. I'd have to work from home to keep an eye on Florcita and Enrique. Yes, I can see this working.

A bank loan is out of the question. We've no guarantees to give. And the banks demand repayment within four months. Carlos says the government is offering low interest loans but they are for peasants with land, and we've sold our holding, so that's that.

President Daniel was once a decent man, tried to see everyone had rice and beans to put on the table, tried to tackle the poverty, but not now. An interest-free loan doesn't exist and when you can't pay back in time, the interest doubles. I know poor folk who've lost everything. No, I'd not go near a bank and never a money lender. The only way is if the whole family helps. Who else would invest in three old ladies?

Folk with money would rather import tacky cheap crafts made in Costa Rica. I'm teaching kids in Los Pipitos how to make *piñatas* and paper flowers. I've shown them how to weave decorative baskets to hold the three different sizes of rum bottles. They look better than the ones in the Masaya craft market and cost next to nothing to make. I collect the banana fronds from the garden and only have to buy the glue and varnish.

I'd be good at running this small business. I learned such a lot working for El Dorado, the shoe manufacturers. We badly needed the money at the time. I started in 1995 and Mum took care of Florcita. I was learning to be a shoemaker, making boots mainly.

I'd been there a few months when the boss called me into her office. I thought last in, first out, I'd be laid off, but not at all. She was full of praise for my work and must have spotted something in me because she asked if I'd like to move on into sales. Maybe she thought I had a gift for this. Anyhow, she asked if I'd go and sell to the supermarkets in Managua, and said that on top of my wage, I'd get a percentage on any sales. With that I immediately said yes.

From that day on I was taking the morning bus from La Concha to Managua to meet with the boss over breakfast, then I was off around the different markets showing our catalogue with shoe samples to shop and stall owners.

Slowly sales started improving and with that, production increased. The boss was delighted and so were the workers. I was doing so well for El Dorado that the boss asked if I'd consider travelling out of town. She asked if I'd go to Matagalpa, León and Granada. It meant being away from home for days at a stretch so I had to ask Mum to step in to care for Florcita. Evita and Hermosa couldn't do it – they were at school – and Enrique wasn't well enough, and when he was he was doing his carpentry.

I went as far as Rivas in the south and all the way to Jinotega in the north. I travelled on the bus with the El Dorado portfolio and a case of shoe samples, going from town to town. I'd book myself into a local guest house and spend the next day seeing different store keepers, becoming quite friendly with some.

I could tell them any detail about the different shoes and boots and their leather quality, and by the end of the week I'd return with a book full of orders. Those three years' sales pushed El Dorado's production up through the roof, and when the boss asked me to take on Chinandega I wasn't surprised. But that was too much. I had to be away by three in the morning and I was stretched, but El Dorado made a pot of gold and at last we had no money problems.

But all that came to an end when Mum passed away. That was seven years ago, in 2001. I haven't worked since because of the kids, but how long could I have kept going at that pace? Life isn't about material gain. I only pray for good health and that we stay close as a family.

# 7 The harvest

*My latest visit to Rosa and her family was in 2013.*

## Rosa

I was in a panic, rushing around looking for help and in the end had to pay some lads. They worked without a break gathering in the beans. They could easily have been ruined. There shouldn't be these torrential downpours; it's the dry season.

Flor offered me the covered area of their garden to dry the beans but I didn't take her up on it because Sara's boyfriend, Emilio, thought her space wasn't big enough. He said to leave the beans to dry on the plot. I brought him plastic sheeting and he stayed there to uncover the beans every time the sun came out. Thankfully after two days the rains subsided.

I've now got the beans stored in the back of the house. I've enough to sell and hopefully will make a little money. My sisters and brothers have all been over for a big bagful each. Dora gave me oranges from their garden and Flor gave me a lot of her squash.

The plot is two kilometres from here, and for Emilio it's much further. He leaves his place at five in the morning and cycles most of the way. It's a tough, rough climb for him. I don't know how he does it and often he's carrying three litres of water. There's no water on the land so he has to take his own.

For two weeks he was staying there, staying overnight on the plot to guard against thieves. Yes, someone could have come to steal the beans. He made himself a shelter and only had his hammock, a lamp and transistor radio, but he had Sara with him. Sara said she was scared at night but went to keep him company. I took him his meals, going by motor taxi to the edge of town, and walked the rest of the way. We've all worked hard towards this harvest. Angélica has been helping too since she's been off work. I don't think I'd have managed without her.

Now that the beans are in, Emilio is putting down compost around the *pitahaya* and later today he'll be fumigating. He bought a barrel of water and brought it to the plot by cart. I don't know where he hired the cart. It all costs. He needs the water to dilute the insecticide. He knows to be very careful with the chemical.

I'm wondering if I should grow more *pitahaya* fruit. I've been thinking about this since I met Hugo last week. I met him on my way to the plot. He was going on further to his holding and we got chatting. I know his sister. He told me he's selling his *pitahaya* to an American, a señor Thompson. Hugo said this American has bought a farm here and is looking to buy all the local growers' *pitahaya* to export. Hugo said this man is providing technical assistance and is buying at a fixed price. That's an attractive proposition when you find prices falling with a good harvest. He said this man is already paying wages to some workers. Hugo offered to take a look at my *pitahaya* and gave me his number so I'm going call him.

I'm thinking also of planting some soya. This isn't the region for it but I've talked to the priest about my idea that maybe I could set up a soya kitchen for the kids going to the primary school.

The holding isn't mine. It belongs to my brother Sergio. Why I have it is because Sergio was worried he'd lose it. He had to re-register the land with the General Properties Registrar. It's a good thing the government is seeing everyone who has land has a deed and can't then be evicted. But Sergio was worried his land might be confiscated because he's been in Costa Rica all these years and had let the land go wild. That's why he asked me to step in and make use of it.

It was very hard work for Emilio to clear the undergrowth. The first year he opened up half the ground and planted corn and beans. He also grew a lot of vegetables, enough to put food on our table. I find Emilio is dependable, he talks everything through with me.

But he might well only stick around for as long as he's with Sara. Emilio is Sara's first boyfriend and Sara is still young and her eyes might well wander!

\* \* \*

Soon after we moved to La Concha I went to see Padre Marlon about Sara. I needed to talk to someone I could trust. Sara had already dropped out of school in Managua and she refused to go to school here. And when she told me she wanted to meet her birth mother I thought the worst: that I might lose her. I'd always been open with her about her mother and she knew exactly where to find her.

I told Padre Marlon all this and he said, 'You're worried Sara will want to stay with her mum and be led astray by her bad ways, but that's so unlikely.' He reassured me, saying that 'Sara's been with you since she was a baby. She can't forget you. You *are* her home.' He read to me a scripture from the Bible about a weak tree producing poor fruit and a strong tree growing good healthy fruit, and told me to have faith that she'd return soon.

But this made it no less painful to see her go. She was only thirteen. I tried holding onto his advice, that she'd come back by her own accord. All I could do was tell her I loved her and ask her to respect herself. It wasn't easy. But you know, she came back home the same day. She said her mother's boyfriend scared her and she didn't feel safe with them.

It wasn't long after that visit to her mother that she took up with Emilio. She met him at his mum's fruit stall by the bus stand. She'd go there to buy fruit and got chatting. When he then started dating her everyone in the family told me to stop fretting, saying I should be happy because Emilio was, and still is, totally smitten with her. And it has lasted; they've been together fourteen months. Emilio's ten years older than her and I think it's lasted this long because he accepts her for how she is, which is pretty untogether. He does all the work and I mean all. He's built them a fine little home. He bought the blocks and timber and constructed the house with his own bare hands. It's needing finishing. Like most men from La Concha, he's a good builder. No doubt he'd have more going for him if he'd learn to read and write. I offered to teach him but he said no, he didn't need that to know carpentry and wiring.

Emilio's leaving soon to go north. He'll be away for three months to pick coffee in Matagalpa. He'll be gone from November to February. Here the coffee is picked within one month and after that there's not much paid work. When Emilio comes back, he says, he'll buy them a proper double bed with springs.

Sara says she doesn't want to have a baby, so that's good. She's made sure of that. She's too young to be with Emilio but how could I stop her? And I can see he cares for her.

If Sara does leave him, and he then stops working on the plot, I'll have to find someone else to help. Also I know Sergio's offer will only last until he can sell. That's what he wants. The thing is, it isn't an attractive buy. The land is far from town and the terrain too steep. That's why it hasn't sold in six years.

All we can do is plant as much as we can for as long as we can. Emilio knows the deal. He's planted for him and Sara a lot of squash and zucchini and they're coming on nicely, so that shows he's keen to stay.

\* \* \*

*She's too young to be with Emilio but how could I stop her?*

Without the food we've grown these past years, we couldn't have managed. Angélica's wages only covered the bills and I'd no income. My pension took two years to sort out because of the trouble I made for myself when I burnt my ID card. I needed to have it to claim my pension. What a run-around but I had to renew it anyway since I changed my residency to here. Renewing it took a whole year, then the next year to sort out my pension.

I was far from the only one. For the past four years, senior citizens have been demanding their pension for all the years they'd paid into the Social Security system. This was a lot of elderly people: some fifteen thousand had paid but hadn't worked the mandatory fourteen years to receive the total pension.

We were asking for no more than our legal right to a partial pension for those years we'd paid. Third Age groups sprung up all over the country, including one in La Concha, which I joined. Every other Saturday we met and, you know me, always ready to scatter those 'wild grass' seeds to help the networking. I was joining what had become a countrywide Third Age movement. The government tried brushing us aside but that only made us protest all the louder. We went to Managua and knocked on Daniel Ortega's door, and we went and talked to the human rights people in their office, and to the representatives in the National Assembly. And we asked them direct: could they live on air like they would have us do? We said that at our age we couldn't find work, our families couldn't afford to feed us, and there was no help for those needing walking frames, medicines or glasses.

In the end President Ortega was forced to make an offer. But what was it? A voucher to come out of the Venezuela Solidarity Fund, like this was Daniel's personal solidarity, thanks to President Chávez of Venezuela. And in exchange he expected us to support his Sandinista candidates.

Daniel could have withdrawn that voucher the next day. Our right to a pension wasn't on the statute books or in the budget. So on we went campaigning and that's when the university students joined us in support of our claim. Together we occupied the Social Security building in Managua and that's when it turned ugly. The police evicted us from the building and the students were attacked, beaten up by thugs. They must have been told what to do, and the police just stood back and watched.

The government was to blame. Who else had hired these thugs and told the police to do nothing? The government got some very bad headlines and everyone was outraged, which only went to strengthen the campaign. Daniel should have known better; we're his generation after all, we know how to stand our ground and we weren't backing down. In the end the government saw no way out. Daniel tried turning this to his advantage with a fanfare of publicity making out he was the good guy all along. But the victory was ours, we'd won our right to our pension, and now I can make ends meet.

The Third Age group is still meeting and everyone's welcome. The group is no way political. My friends only took white flags for peace to the Sandinista July 19 celebration in Managua. I didn't go though. Yes, I've made some good friends in this group and renewed others from my school days. I've been put on the spot a couple of times: 'Don't you remember me, we were in the same class?' And then I realize I'm talking to an old school friend.

* * *

The best thing about moving back to La Concha is having the family nearby. Life is fine now, though at the start the move was unsettling for the children. Padre Marlon helped Darío a lot. Darío needed to occupy his time and when he didn't get a job in the Free Trade Zone, Padre Marlon put me in touch with the centre Darío now goes to. He loves it there; it's like another family for him.

Darío has been given the responsibility for their kitchen garden. He tells me about the plants they grow, how they're coming on and how they're used in their meals at the centre. He works along-side their gardener, whom I've met; he's a kind man, teaching Darío about organic horticulture. Darío likes the carpentry classes too and playing volleyball. He's given a small wage to cover his travel expenses. The youngsters enrol from fifteen years of age and can stay there for as long as they want. Yes, he's very happy there. He's the first to arrive in the mornings.

I'm up before him at five to prepare his breakfast and packed lunch. Then Richie and Iván get up for their breakfast before going to school.

I wouldn't have it any other way. Flor, Dora and I are all caring for our grandkids – Flor is minding her two and Dora her three and me Angélica's two. That's what put paid to our idea of the kids' clothes shop. We grannies are doing a double shift, like it was for Mum, and for her mum. We grannies are all looking after our grandchildren. Home was always with the patter of tiny feet.

Helping the boys with their homework really makes a difference. For the last three years Iván has been top of his class. There he is, in that photo, wearing the Sash for Excellence. Richie's bright too. It's his behaviour that lets him down. He can get so angry. Angélica and I went with him to see the psychologist from Los Pipitos. He said he thought Richie's trouble probably wasn't down to any one thing. He thought Angélica's separation from his father and her being away working a lot when Richie was a baby, and also him seeing Mateo being violent, would all contribute to his behaviour. Richie saw how Mateo treated his mother. I think that's why he had these tantrums. Richie refused to call Mateo Dad. I told Mateo, 'Richie knows you're not his father. If you wanted him to feel you are, then show him you care.'

Richie knows I love him but I can see how he must have missed his mother when he was a baby. He needed more of her attention. His behaviour has improved a lot since starting school. He's completed third grade. Before he started school I spoke to Padre Marlon and I know he made sure Richie's teacher understood. From Richie's first day there Padre Marlon treated him like his little helper and during the break-times Richie knew he could always go and see the secretary. She always made him welcome.

He's been getting good marks in computer science and English, but he finds maths and social studies hard. He started social studies in fourth grade. He's learning about Nicaragua's history and geology and the road to Central America's independence. He likes the class, it's just that he won't take any notes. I've told him he has to write down what the teacher says. Angélica is now helping him to catch up. She's taken over from me.

Having Angélica at home is giving me a bit of a holiday. I'm doing less since she's been off work. She was suspended a month ago. It wasn't anything she'd done. The trouble is her boss. Her superintendent tried to involve Angélica in her schemes, telling Angélica to give her kickbacks. But one thing Angélica isn't is corrupt and when she wouldn't comply, her boss wanted to get rid of her. It's incredible, her boss falsified Angélica's police records to make out she was incompetent.

Angélica has a lawyer paid for by the Police Force who's dealing with the allegation and today Angélica is meeting with him and her police superiors. Her lawyer will present the evidence proving this superintendent forged Angélica's signature. I've no doubt Angélica will be cleared, but she thinks her boss won't be removed. Angélica says more likely she'll be the one to move. She wants to transfer anyway to Masaya to be nearer home and have more time with the boys. She wouldn't want to work in La Concha. It's too close to home and there's hardly any crime here.

* * *

In truth her job is the least of her troubles. Mateo is her headache. She'd no idea what she was letting herself in for. It was only after she married him that she found out about him dealing drugs. That was the real reason why he was in Costa Rica. He only came back after Iván was born.

She first met Mateo when his mum died. They got married way too soon. And now that they are, Mateo says that's how they're going to stay. But they've never lived together. Whenever she's spent any time with him it's ended in him beating her and her running away. Supposedly he can't control himself. He's diabetic like his mother was and maybe that causes his mood swings. Angélica somehow seems tuned into his erratic behaviours, but that's no way to live, to be on edge all the time. He can change in an instant from being an angel to a total thug.

I won't have him here. He used to visit when we were living in Managua until he stole money of mine. He was another reason to move to La Concha, and I won't have him coming here looking for Angélica. Mateo is why I've left the house to Darío. I talked this through with Carlos and Laura and they agreed. You see, as long as Angélica remains married, the house could pass on to him. Ah no, Angélica has no future with Mateo. She's much more relaxed living here. She knows she can rely on me to look after the boys and knows Mateo's family wouldn't do that.

Bad things have happened. Mateo followed Angélica onto the bus one evening and pulled her off at a gas station and started punching her. Thanks to two men she got away. They grabbed hold of Mateo and she called the police. Mateo was in prison for two weeks.

She said she didn't want any more to do with him but a month later I heard her talking to him on her mobile phone. I think she's frightened to say no. This was last Christmas and she left here with the boys. All I got out of her was that Mateo wanted to see the boys. My heart sank watching her pack the hold-all, worried she was leaving for good. But the very next day she called around six in the evening. 'Mum, it's me. I'm leaving Managua. I've the boys with me. Please will you come and meet us at the bus stop?'

*At last Angélica is filing for divorce*

'Yes, fine, I'll be there.'

At seven thirty she called again to say they were nearing La Concha. Darío and I met them off the bus and what a state she was in: exhausted, dirty, her hair all over the place. Walking back home Richie said, 'Mateo was drunk.' They'd seen him drunk and no doubt more. And they were both starving hungry, the little ones.

When the boys had gone to bed, Angélica told me Mateo had no money and was out of his mind. She said once he started on her, she told the boys to get out and she fought him off to get away and ran down the street with the boys. Again she said, never again. That's another reason why Angélica needs to be transferred from Managua, to put distance between them. Too many bad things like that have happened.

At last Angélica is filing for divorce. She had to call Mateo to ask him to a meeting with the lawyer. She told me afterwards what he'd said: 'Sure we can meet the lawyer; that's if you're still alive.' He's dangerous. I told her if she doesn't go and report

*They'll be fine*

this, then I'll go myself. And to think she's a policewoman. I suspect his gang calls her too, threatening her to do what she's told, otherwise something bad might happen to me or Darío or to Richie. Mateo doesn't care for Richie, not being his father. Angélica hasn't said this to me but that's what I think, that she's frightened he'll do something to us.

Mateo is an ace operator. He's joined the Sandinista Youth Organization and is supposedly in charge of 'road safety' in the *barrio* where he lives. That organization is meant to be fighting against exactly what he does: drug dealing and delinquency. How did she fall for this guy?

All I know about Mateo's family is that he's their only boy and he has six sisters. His father was a carpenter by trade, retired now, and very into the Evangelical Church.

When we've talked about Mateo, Angélica has said she can see how his controlling, macho aggression is like the flipside of him falling apart on drink and drugs, and she's right there. She wants so much that her boys do not follow his bad example and wants to find the right balance of giving them discipline and freedom. I think being here in La Concha with us and the family, they'll be fine. They like to help sweep the floor and they fold their clothes away. Richie said his teacher has both the girls and boys keeping the school tidy. They all have their little chores to do like cleaning the windows, emptying the waste baskets, and wiping the board. And their teacher also told them to help at home. And the sports coach treats the girls and boys exactly the same. In these ways the old roles of men and women will change.

But what I also know is far too many children grow up feeling unwanted. Really, when I think about Mateo all I see is a little insecure boy. His insecurity is something I see in so many youngsters and I can't put it down to the unemployment. It goes way beyond that. Think about the impact of so many dying in the fight against Somoza in the seventies. Forty thousand children were left orphaned to be brought up by some relative. And all the widows, all the single mums, had to get on and work, and leave their babies with a sister or granny or maybe they'd have a nursery. That's what I'm saying: too many children grew up feeling unloved. And just when we were making life a little better in the eighties under the Sandinista government, the Contra war took over, bringing more grief and more mums being widowed and more babies left to be minded by whomever while they tried to make ends meet.

And then from the nineties onwards, thousands upon thousands were put out of work and so forced to migrate in search of jobs in Costa Rica, Mexico, the United States, even as far as Spain. Like Pilar and William, they left their three kids with their Granny Dora. Anyone can see their older boy feels lost and abandoned and takes his hurt out on Dora. Today's youngsters need a lot of help. This insecurity among the youth stems from decades of violence and upheaval.

Yes, we women are the ones left to cope. That's why so many came together, and that's what brought change for many women, by being together. At the very least we took stock of all this to want something better. There are many women's organizations that have done such a lot to make this happen, networking in the *barrios*. That's why I keep my pocketful of 'wild grass' seeds, to scatter wherever it can grow. It's networking that kept my spirit up. I've still got that. I've been very fortunate knowing the people I do. When I'm in Managua I go and see how they're doing in the *barrio*, keeping the sports and drama activities going for the kids.

Channel Ten puts on a programme covering the kind of things they're dealing with in the barrio, like, 'Why youngsters become delinquent' or 'Behind today's violence'. The last programme was, 'Why Nicaraguans binge-drink' and a lad interviewed was saying that at his end-of-year school party, three classmates got drunk and went to Tiscapa lagoon in Managua for a swim. He said they were all out of their minds and that's why the three had drowned. He was saying alcohol had to be off limits in schools. I'd say off limits everywhere. I blame a lot on the ads telling youngsters, 'Rum is for Real Men'.

Recently there's been on TV a campaign to warn youngsters against ads targeting them to 'travel abroad for exciting new jobs'. They'd uncovered that many kids run away chasing dreams of a good job abroad only to end up trapped into prostitution or drugs. And so often these are kids running away from families who are living in permanent crisis. And this is what I'm saying, this is all because of decades of turmoil and poverty.

It makes me want to pray; pray for the love of humanity, to fill our hearts with love, to keep strong to be able to carry on. There is goodness in our humanity, and in there lies our dignity, our grace. Being poor is never the problem. Being poor isn't hard, it's when you lose your dignity that's the problem. Just think about how life could be. There really is enough for everyone to be comfortable. If everyone could just take that to heart and give to their neighbour, let it be only a *tortilla* with cheese, what a place this could be. Life can be good as long as you face up to the difficulties you meet on the way and don't run away.

I was invited to a wedding here in La Concha and I thought how odd the priest asking the bride and groom to be faithful and remain a couple, and look after their children together to enjoy seeing them grow up and to be blessed with grandchildren. He came across as if pleading with them, as if this was so unlikely to happen.

But he was telling the truth. Most I know are in rocky relationships. Angélica thinks I don't know the half of what Mateo is up to, and I prefer it that way. She talks more to Laura; being sisters, they share a lot more. Laura doesn't tell me much either. She makes out she does exactly what she pleases, going here, going there. I'm glad she's using her skills in her job. She's been on an economics course run by her employer, the Agricultural Credit Cooperative, and she just finished another short course to bring her up to date on using her computer. But I know how things really are with Heraldo. He takes off at the weekends and she'll be on the phone three, four times to him, saying she wants him home. And he's no better; if she's not home when he calls, he asks her to go back. That's why their older boy, Allan, stays with his grandparents. He doesn't even come home at the weekends since he found out about his dad. He heard the two of them arguing about Heraldo's other woman. Allan says he has no time to come home anyway, what with all his studies and sports he does and that's good. It's their younger one, Gabriel, I worry about. He's a daddy's boy, goes everywhere with Heraldo. And Laura thinks that's OK, she thinks Heraldo will drink less if his son is with him. It's her way to fret less but for sure this will be replayed when the boy grows up.

I think Laura does have a limit on what she'll put up with and if it does come to a divorce, I'm sure Heraldo will be decent enough to let her keep the house. It's in both their names. I think the law would fall in her favour anyway with the youngest still living at home.

I only know all this about Heraldo through Angélica. And Laura is the one who tells me about Angélica and her cousin Myrna. I try and stay out of Myrna's troubles since she split up from Danielo. Myrna's dad was never there for her so it's good she feels at home with Danielo's mum. At least she feels loved by her mother-in-law. She was there when Myrna gave birth and has helped with bringing up her two boys.

\* \* \*

I'd talk about all these concerns with Padre Marlon and that always helped. He always gave good advice. When he was due to move on to a new diocese, no one wanted him to go. Padre Marlon still had a big project on the go, the new secondary school. The town's council, the school and the church were working together and had drawn up a plan. So everyone signed a petition asking for his post to be extended for another five years and we were very happy when Archbishop Brenes agreed to this.

Padre Marlon was warm-hearted and committed to the Lord's work. He had no time for anything other than church work. He only ever socialized at wedding receptions. I never heard a bad word spoken against him.

It's been a year since Padre Marlon disappeared. For days no one knew where he had gone, and we all were worried. Then we heard the terrible news that he had been killed. At first I couldn't believe it. It still is a mystery why this happened. No one knows the motive behind this crime. One of his murderers was caught and is serving a thirty-year jail sentence but the man never confessed to why he killed Padre Marlon, only that yes, he had done it. I think he must have been paid by someone to keep silence. He didn't do this alone.

This was all very upsetting. The boys still talk about Padre Marlon; they miss him, especially Richie. We are still grieving.

The Sunday after Padre Marlon's death, Monsignor Leopoldo Brenes came to say Mass. He tried to console us. Richie and Iván were crying throughout Mass, the whole family was. Monsignor Brenes spoke of God's message being one of love and forgiveness but that wasn't how I felt. When he asked the congregation to let Jesus Christ into our hearts and to show compassion, I felt if we all have a right to life, then why had Padre Marlon died this way, and how he must have suffered.

I miss Padre Marlon. Nothing like that had ever happened here, not for a long time. What violence there is, is hidden behind doors, like family troubles, a lover's tiff. There was a drunk found dead in the cemetery but he wasn't murdered, and a long time ago a child was killed. Like Angélica says, she'd be bored if she was in the Police Force here.

Padre Marlon always gave sound advice. I told him about our dispute over the inheritance and he told me I needed to see a lawyer. It still hasn't been sorted out. The original property deed we know grandma gave to Mum hasn't been found. It probably disintegrated. It's over forty years since grandma died and the lawyer who drew up that deed is long since gone too. But Mum had made her intentions clear to all of us. 'I'm leaving the land to Marcos, Ana and Rosa, and Guillermo is to inherit the house because he helped build it. Ana, Rosa and Marcos will divide the land equally.' And we were all present when she said this.

Mum gave Guillermo the house and wanted him to see to its upkeep. But you know, Guillermo had had enough of bailing out Ana. He'd had enough of her man, Lucho. All these years Lucho has done nothing other than build a frame for his squash. That's all they eat, morning, noon and night – squash – and that's what keeps him there, his food.

It's three years since Guillermo gave Ana the house in exchange for the land Mum had given her. Soon after that, she asked him to return her plot, which he did and at a token price. But three years on, Ana still hasn't paid him.

Ana thinks she deserves everything after caring for Mum in her old age. But she forgets how we all gave what we could towards her care. She said to Flor that I'm the lucky one to have a pension and my own home. Flor put her right, 'That's nothing to do with luck. For years Rosa has worked hard to earn her pension and have a home.' Ana likes to think I've no problems and don't need that land. If I had the ground she has around this house here, Richie and Iván wouldn't be out playing on the street and I'd have lemongrass, oregano and cinnamon growing in my own medicinal garden.

No matter what differences we have, we're still family. I've always had more get-up-and-go than Ana. I suppose out of all my sisters I'm closest to Flor. And I've a lot of respect for Carlos. Carlos agrees, like all my brothers and sisters, we must sort out this mess with Ana. He was right too to tell Indiana that any more children would be more poverty. Ana's daughter Indiana is already a grandma when she's only a girl herself. She's a girl with a girl with a baby girl. That's another mess.

Carlos only comes here now and again. He's too busy to get away, Prof. Carlos. That's what they call him in Matiguás. I'll visit him when I get the chance.

He's stuck to his principles and stayed loyal to the Sandinista Party. He talks still about their founding values, as if nothing has changed. He campaigned in their 2012 elections in Matiguás and after the Sandinistas won, he's been non-stop covering both jobs: his agricultural job and his responsibilities on the Municipal Council. The Matiguás Council has joined forces with the Liberals, and Carlos is busy promoting the government's Decent Roof housing project, and the Zero Hunger project that gives out one sow, hens and a cow to small-scale farmers. Carlos says that women often are the beneficiaries. But to my mind, each cow comes at a price. Many folk you talk to think the same as me, that Ortega and his wife, Rosario Murillo, are becoming another ruling dynasty. Certainly their billboards along the highways give that impression. Their message is to humbly accept that they're the ones in charge.

We use that word 'humility' a lot in Nicaragua and for me it has two completely different meanings. There's the social, political meaning that is to accept what you're given and ask for no more, which is the message Ortega and Murillo put out. Then there is the spiritual meaning which is all about being honest and tolerant of others, appreciating the life you have, and not wasting time on wanting what will only bring you discontent. Like, what's the point in me wanting a car? Wanting one would only lead me to convince myself I actually need one. And say I got one, how could I afford the endless petrol? That'd be plain foolish. Humility in that sense means avoiding being pretentious. It means to do what you can by your own efforts and defend your right to live a dignified life, and not bow your head saying 'yes sir' to the powers that be.

That's the political system I think we have. It wants us to bow our heads, especially if you're after a job in the state sector. A nephew of mine is applying for a job in the Customs Division of Import Taxation, and he knows his application won't be accepted without an endorsement of his political credentials. He has trained in this but won't get through the door without this political authorization. It's a formal letter of recommendation stating you're honest and conscientious. I've read this, a load of flowery words. How can his local Sandinista rep sign this if he doesn't know my nephew? How can he say my nephew is honest and responsible? This 'endorsement' is basically telling my nephew to be hypocritical, to say 'I'm a Sandinista' in order to get the letter. The letter has nothing to do with being a Sandinista, it's about conceding that Murillo-Ortega are his leaders and he depends on them to get *their* state jobs.

Of course I can see good things happening too. Sara's only back at school thanks to the new educational programmes and grants that are now available. I'm pleased about that. The new national educational English programme is another good development, even if it's only come about because of this famous interoceanic canal project. Ortega has signed over this project to the Chinese, but on the back of that, youngsters are learning English. It might help them find jobs with the overseas companies coming to dig out the canal. Also tourism, information technology is said, will grow and bring more jobs. This Sandinista government is a real mixed bag.

Look how much Carlos has contributed. They are achievements that are real and beautiful. He started out as a student teaching in the 1980 Literacy Crusade and from then to now, he's worked to improve the lives of folk in Matiguás.

And his children are all ahead thanks to their upbringing. Carlos's girl Mónica is a business administrator and their youngest is a computer programmer. The middle one, Carlito, went for some time to Costa Rica to work in the building trade, but he's back now because building work has picked up in Matiguás since the Sandinistas won the last elections. Mónica is home too and has a job using her business skills.

She's twenty-seven. When I asked her if she wanted to marry she said, 'Why would I want that? That'd be a step back.' She's single and independent and likes her social life. And that's a good thing. I've always believed in being independent, for all women, not just for me.

Yes, all my life I've kept to my own path. I was lucky never to slip up or take the wrong path. I'd have been only poorer in myself if I'd done that and run away from my responsibilities.

## Latin America Bureau (LAB)

Latin America Bureau (Research and Action) Limited (LAB) is an independent publishing and research organization. A registered charity, based in the UK, LAB provides news, analysis and information on Latin America, reporting consistently from the perspective of the region's poor, oppressed or marginalized communities and social movements. LAB brings an alternative, critical awareness and understanding of Latin America to readers throughout the English-speaking world.

Founded in 1977, LAB is widely known as the publisher of over 150 books and operates a website, updated regularly, which carries news and analysis on Latin America and reports from more than 40 partners and correspondents in the region (www.lab.org.uk). LAB distributes a free e-newsletter to subscribers in many countries. You can sign up for the newsletter by clicking 'Subscribe' on the www.lab.org.uk home page.

In 2015 LAB entered into a publishing partnership with Practical Action Publishing Ltd, who will distribute all LAB titles, new and old, through www.developmentbookshop.com.

## Latest LAB titles

*Faces of Latin America 4th Edition* by Duncan Green, with Sue Branford
*Brazil Inside Out: People, politics and culture 2nd Edition* by Jan Rocha and Francis McDonagh
*The Nicaragua Grand Canal: Economic miracle or folie de grandeur?* by Russell White
*Brazil under the Workers' Party: From euphoria to despair* by Sue Branford and Jan Rocha
*Argentina: the Kirchners and the rise and fall of left populism* by Marcela López Levy and Nick Caistor
*K* by Bernardo Kucinski

Subscription to the LAB collection can be accessed through www.practicalactionpublishing.org/digital-collections

A full list of LAB titles is available on www.developmentbookshop.com/latin-america-bureau-titles

The complete catalogue of LAB titles can be downloaded from www.practicalactionpublishing.org/new-catalogue